SINFUL *temptation*

LONDON HALE

LONDON HALE

*Dedicated to Joseph Mortimer Granville,
without whom hysterical paroxysm would be that
much harder to achieve.*

chapter one

NOAH

I WAS USED to the older women of my congregation gossiping after the Sunday services. What I wasn't used to was making a wrong turn and practically falling right into those half-whispered conversations.

"It's just obscene."

Yup. Totally made a wrong turn.

"It is. Poor Prudence must be rolling over in her grave."

"She sells dildos in there."

My entire body flinched, my need to escape growing. I just had to disappear into the parking lot. It wasn't too far. So long as they kept talking and didn't notice me…

"Marge," Norma hissed, rebuking the head of the ladies' council.

"Oh, Norma. What? That's what they are.

They're called dildos…fake penises. Am I right, Pastor Noah?"

Shit… I didn't want to be involved in their discussion, but I couldn't ignore them. No matter how much I wanted to.

"Well, Marge, I do believe you're right. They're called"—*Lord, help me*—"dildos."

Marge, a well-rounded lady with hair as gray as a stormy sky, elbowed her friend and coconspirator. "See, Norma? That's what she's selling in there. Fake penises."

I tried to leave them to it, to slip toward the little house on the far side of the church parking lot where I lived. Sadly, they turned as if to include me in their conversation about sex toys. I had a busy Sunday to get to—I had a few minutes to grab a quick lunch before Bible study began, then the grounds committee was turning over the flowerbeds for the season, and finally, the choir leader wanted a meeting to discuss hymn options for our Christmas season. My day was filled with church responsibilities. Tonight, like all nights, it seemed, was wide open. Empty. Except for my fantasies of *her*. Owner of the store they scorned. The one they shunned because she embraced her sexuality.

I'd really like to embrace her sexuality.

Marge huffed again. "If you ask me, the city council never should have let her have her business there. It's just…wrong."

I would have disagreed, but I'd learned early on not to argue with the old ladies in Marge's clique. I really wished I would have avoided them altogether. Why had I chosen to come out the front entrance, again? Oh, right. Because of the adult toy store across the street. Well, the owner of the adult toy store across the street.

Norma hummed, pulling my attention from my current obsession. "I can't believe she turned that nice tea shop into such a place."

"It's just so shameful," Marge said for what had to be the hundredth time since I'd been called to this little church in Temperance Falls. Shameful, deviant, obscene, wrong—different words, same meaning behind them. There was a group of older ladies within my church who hated that the granddaughter of a deceased friend of theirs had taken a cozy, Christian bookstore and tea shop and turned it into…Sin.

"I'm not sure I understand why you allow her to park in our lot, Pastor Noah," Norma said, on a roll as she had been the past few Sundays. "It just seems so…dirty."

Dirty were the thoughts I had about the owner of the shop, Harper Davis. Thoughts of what she did late at night up in that apartment of hers above her store, of what she would—or wouldn't—wear once the shades were drawn and she was alone. Thoughts of what I wanted to do to her if she could ever see me as more than just the neighborhood pastor. But I couldn't tell the old ladies that.

"Miss Davis has no parking lot and can't park on the street past ten. It would be callous of me not to allow her to park her car in our lot, seeing as she's our neighbor and all. I wouldn't want her to have to walk over to the community lot late at night."

"But there are…pictures in that car. Naked pictures."

All thoughts of staying calm and rational with my congregation flew out of my mind. Naked pictures? When I'd offered Harper a parking spot in the church lot, it had been with the understanding that she not leave any of her business paraphernalia in the car itself. I could hold off the blue-hairs on the basis of safety and concern for our neighbor, but only if she played by the rules.

"Naked pictures?"

"Go look. They're all over the back seat." Norma turned back to Marge, whispering about the devil and filth and more things than I wanted to deal with. I just wanted to eat a quick sandwich before I had to start the rest of my day. As was my usual Sunday morning routine, I'd gotten up at five to begin prep for the day. I was tired, cranky, and in need of one damned day where old ladies stopped complaining about Harper.

Still, to be a good leader of my congregation, I headed over to the car in question. The one I allowed to park in the side lot more for my own peace of mind than Harper's. She had never asked for the spot; I'd offered it after watching her walk alone through the dark streets one evening. The thought of her out on a date was bad enough—the thought of her in danger when she was coming home from it was too much for me to deal with. I'd gone over to her shop the next morning and offered her parking privileges in the church lot. It was just the neighborly thing to do, after all.

The car windows glinted in the midday sun, and I had to shade my eyes to see inside. There were naked pictures, all right. Of men. A blue file folder sat on the back seat, its contents strewn across the seat and floor. Naked men. Posing. Oil-covered. Hard. They looked like some sort of advertisement for an upcoming event, dates and times written in white across the bottom. Didn't matter. There were photos of naked men in her car.

My patience snapped.

I stormed across the street, ready to break. A sandwich. That was all I'd wanted. A simple sandwich. And now I had to deal with an affronted Marge, with Norma saying things like dildo, and naked men in the back seat of Harper's car. The only naked man who should be in her back seat was me…even if she didn't know that yet.

I yanked open the door to Sin just as someone else was exiting. Two someones. People I recognized.

"Pastor Noah." Joshua Hutton—local doctor, widower, and single dad—gave me a smile that should have calmed my ire. Should have, but did not. "I gotta say, I wasn't anticipating running into you here."

I bit back the growl his words incited. Typical—I was a pastor and, therefore, asexual to the people around me.

His nanny, Bailey, a beautiful young woman I'd

noticed looking at him with more than just employee respect, stood beside him. The two had a relaxed air about them, a certain body language that spoke of intimacy. Perhaps it was how close they stood, or the fact that she almost seemed to be leaning into his side. Whatever it was, that sense of *more* they exuded only pissed me off. I wanted that…always had.

Do not covet. Do not covet. Dammit, I was definitely coveting.

"Mr. Hutton. Miss Effingham." I tried to nod, tried to control the anger in my voice. The irritation. The disappointment. "Please excuse me. I need to speak to—"

"Pastor No," Harper called from deeper in the store, her voice causing my cock to come to life. The woman herself appeared, and I almost came right there on the spot. Dark, wavy hair set in some old pinup style, blue eyes that practically devoured everything she looked at, and lips… I could speak for hours on the glory of her thick, plush lips. Lips that were made for kissing, for biting…for fucking. Everything about her was a turn-on, every action, word, and look an invitation it seemed. And she knew it. "You just can't stay away from Sin, can you?"

No, I couldn't. Not when she was the one running it. Especially not when she was looking at me with that sly smile as if I hadn't caught the double entendre of her words.

Still, there were people watching us. I had to play my part as the asexual pastor. No matter how much that was a lie.

"Miss Davis, I've asked you repeatedly to call me Noah. Like the rest of the congregation."

Those lips of hers—painted a shiny burgundy today, which matched her blouse—quirked up in a smile that only made me move closer. "Ah, but I'm not part of your congregation, now am I?"

No. She wasn't. But that wouldn't stop me. Joshua and Bailey disappeared out the door, leaving me alone with Harper. In Sin.

"You have pictures of naked men in the back seat of your car. I've asked you not to leave your shop paraphernalia where the congregation can see it. Seeing anything related to sex"—fuck, just saying the word in such close proximity to her made me hard as stone—"upsets them."

But Harper wasn't one to be pushed around. Which was something I liked about her.

She waved a dismissive hand and rolled her eyes. "They're just flyers. Those old biddies can't handle anything. Seriously, when do you think any of them last got laid?"

Oh, for Chri—

"I can't say I've ever thought about the sex lives of my congregation. Now, about those pictures—"

"That's too bad," she said, completely ignoring my concerns over the photos. Again. "It's a game I like to play as I watch everyone walk by. You can tell a lot about people by their reaction to the shop, you know. And those harpies? I bet Nixon was in office the last time any of them got some action. I couldn't imagine."

Harper bit her lip, her eyes staring just off to the side as if in thought. As if truly contemplating the sex lives of women more than twice her age. She raised her hand, an almost unconscious act, and began running her fingers along her collarbone. Back and forth, back and forth.

I was fascinated.

The drape of her blouse hinted at the softness hidden underneath the fabric, the deep red color contrasting perfectly with her pale skin. Back and forth, back and forth—she kept me captivated. Hypnotized. Until all I could do was stare, all I could think of was where those fingers would go next. All I wanted…was to touch.

Those fingers broke me.

"And what about me?" I asked, still staring, hard as stone and aching for some sort of touch. Some sort of physical sensation from her. The lightest brush of her skin on mine would wreck me forever. I knew it. And still, I hungered for it.

"You?"

"Yes. What do you see when I walk by?"

She stalked closer, her loose-hipped gait making everything on her body sway. The woman was pure sex—all soft and sinful—and she knew it. Used it to her advantage when it suited her. She didn't stop until she was right in front of me. Almost touching.

And then she touched.

She slowly raised her hand, almost defying the laws of time and space. It seemed to take hours for her to reach the collar of my shirt, the style I insisted on wearing every Sunday. A slight tickle at the front of my throat told me she'd made contact with my bow tie, and I'd never been more jealous of a piece of fabric.

"You work so hard to stay all buttoned up, don't you?" she said, her voice low and sultry. "But is that who you really are? Or is it just a show you put on?" She inched ever closer, those high tits of hers brushing against my chest. Their firmness making me want to grab them, bite them, suck the tips until she begged for more.

When she was right up against me, rising up on the balls of her feet to bring her lips to my ear, when she had me completely under her spell, she whispered, "What would you be like out of this costume, Pastor No?"

Done. I was done. Forget holding back or being subtle. She wanted to tease me? Fine. I could tease right back. "Are you sure you're ready to find out, Miss Davis?"

I took a step into her, one hand gripping her waist so she couldn't retreat, unable to resist her for a second more. She followed suit, inching back even as I tracked her, looking me right in the eye as she laughed. Her reaction would have been insulting if it didn't make my cock twitch.

"Oh, honey, I think we both know you wouldn't want to take this for a spin on your first ride."

I blinked. Twice. First *what?* So that's what she thought of me—that I was some virgin preacher who had no idea what to do with a woman? That I was inexperienced, and she'd have to teach me a thing or two? I bet she could, even though I was far from virginal. This would be fun.

I leaned closer, letting my lips come right to the edge of her ear. Almost touching her. And then I whispered, "Who said you'd be my first ride?"

She physically recoiled, staring up at me with those huge blue eyes that had haunted me from the moment we'd met. She gave me a solid once-over. Appraising me. Which was fine, because I was doing the same to her.

"What?" I asked with a shrug, taking another step closer to her. Practically grinning when she tried to take a step back. "Did you really think—"

A clock chimed, and Harper's sultry smile reappeared, though it was a lot less sure at that point. "I think that's your cue, Father."

Stupid busy Sundays. I wasn't ready to let her go, though. Not yet. Not now that I had her attention. Not now that I'd gotten my very first touch. "Do you have to wear blouses with such revealing necklines? It's a distraction. And I'm not a virgin."

"Yes. I do. I'll wear whatever the hell I want. But it's good to know you don't approve. I'll be sure to wear it more often." She tugged her shirt a little lower, smoothing the silky fabric over her waist. Pulling it tight across her breasts. "And you might as well be a virgin. Hell, you might as well be a priest."

Was that disappointment in those wicked eyes of hers? I licked my lips, imagining the taste of hers. Wondering how soft they would be on my skin. How tight when wrapped around my cock. This woman released something inside me I hadn't even known was there, but now that she had, I refused to be caged again. I wanted her. Had since the first moment I'd laid eyes on her. I just had to convince her to take the chance.

I moved back, grabbing her hand to pull her with me. She seemed almost shocked by that—by the fact that I could be a gentleman. What kind of men had she dated?

Never mind. I didn't want to know.

"You know the difference between a priest and a pastor?" I asked as I headed for the door.

"Different faiths, of course."

"True, but that's not where I was going. Priests take a vow of celibacy. Pastors follow the guidelines of the faiths they preach." I pulled the door open, glancing once more at the sultry siren who had no idea what she was in for. "We nondenominational pastors follow wherever the Lord takes us. Today, he brought me to Sin…and to you. I doubt this will be the last time he puts us on the same path. Good day, Miss Davis."

chapter two

HARPER

HOURS HAD PASSED since Noah had come for a visit. Well, *visit* was putting it mildly. If it had been anyone else who'd stopped by, I'd have said it was a solid fifteen minutes of foreplay. But this was Pastor No… As in, hands off, don't touch, no one is getting into those pants.

Who said you'd be my first ride?

I wasn't proud of the fact that just remembering those words on his tongue had my nipples going tight, my belly clenching. My body was *readying* itself for…what, exactly? Because if one thing was true, it was that Noah was a pastor. Vow of celibacy or not, there was no way he was going to fuck around just for the hell of it—or at all—before marriage. And if there was one thing I absolutely wasn't interested in, it was marriage.

Since the store was mostly empty—as it usually was at this time on a Sunday—I took a seat in front of the window at the small table and chairs there, the only remaining pieces from when this place had been my late grandmother's Christian bookstore and tea shop. If anyone would support the marriage of me to the dear pastor, it'd be her. Fucking with him by purposely egging him on, hoping to push him over the edge? *That* she wouldn't be too happy with. It certainly wasn't very Christian of me.

When she'd died last year, her will declaring I receive this building across from one of the local churches as a means to "bring me back to Jesus," I'd just about passed on it. I'd been off living—and enjoying—my life away from the overbearing "love" my dear grandmother used to smother me with. The power struggle between her and my far-too-young mother had been suffocating, each using me as a means to get back at the other. Which was exactly why I'd gotten the hell out of dodge as soon as I'd been legal.

And yet here I was, back in my hometown. Causing trouble.

I slid my gaze out the window toward the building across the street, which was, as always, a magnet for my eyes. Okay, not the building. The *man*.

Noah stood outside, shovel in hand as he worked on the flowerbeds in front of the church. His dark hair was messier than usual, the slight curl making the strands go this way and that the only thing wild about him.

A group of older men surrounded him, supervising. The grounds committee. I snorted at that, knowing the only person over there who ever did any work was Noah himself. That was proved by his disheveled appearance. Disheveled…and completely fucking hot, even in the ridiculously frumpy clothes he chose to wear around his congregation. His should-not-have-been-hot-but-totally-was bow tie was gone—probably so as not to get it dirty—but the rest of him was the same as it'd been earlier today.

Honestly, I'd never seen someone pull off a short-sleeved button-up shirt and pleated—yes, *pleated*—khakis like Noah did. He did all he could to try to cover up every ounce of his body, but it still shone through. Especially when he bent over like that, his biceps flexing against the confines of his short sleeves, his sculpted ass showcased in those proper pants.

Who said you'd be my first ride?

Goddammit, I couldn't get those words out of my head. Or how the whispered breath of them had ghosted over my ear, making me shudder. How his lips had been so close, I could've sworn they'd brushed against me at one point. How his body had pressed right up against mine, tight and toned and…*hard.* Yeah, he'd been hard—there was no doubt about that. Noah was hiding a lot under those frumpy clothes, and if his words were anything to go by, it was more than just a fuckhot body.

I shook myself out of my daze, needing to get

back on sure-footing. This wasn't the kind of game I played—at least, not unless I was the one with the upper hand. And that was exactly what I needed to regain.

Glancing down at my outfit—the one he'd deemed inappropriate—I smiled. If he wanted to play, we'd play. But he better buckle the fuck up, because he was in a league with the big girls now.

After making a quick stop off in my office to rid myself of something I definitely didn't need, I called out to my current help, Chris, that I'd be right back.

He pushed his glasses up the bridge of his nose, laughing from his perch behind the counter. "You're going to give one of those old men a heart attack, Harper."

"But what a way to go, huh?" With a smile and a wink, I pulled on the handle of the door and headed out into the unusually warm fall day. Hand over my eyes to block the bright sun, I called out as I crossed the street. "You fellas sure are working hard today, aren't you?"

I had my eyes locked on Marv, the leader of the grounds committee and husband to one of the old biddies, but made sure to keep Noah in my line of sight. He paused in his movements, his head tilting up to face me. I wouldn't look at him, though. Not yet.

"Harper, nice to see you out today," Marv said, his eyes taking a slow perusal down my body, lingering on my breasts as he licked his lips. Wonder what his wife of forty years would think about him eye-fucking other women. Christian, my ass.

Still, I smiled, placing my hand on his forearm as I shot him and his friends a bright smile. "I could use some of your muscles over at my place. Those great big planters out front are so heavy! Think you all could give me a hand?"

"I've offered my services on numerous occasions, Miss Davis," Noah said before anyone else was able to answer. "I'd be more than happy to move those planters once I'm done here."

I spared him the briefest glance, because God knew if I looked at him for any longer, he was going to have the upper hand again. Totally unacceptable. "Yeah, well"—I shrugged and gave Marv's forearm a light pat—"maybe I'd prefer these other gentlemen to you."

Marv and his buddies laughed good-naturedly, but I couldn't pay much attention to them. Not when I'd made the mistake of turning my gaze to Noah. Not when he narrowed his eyes, his jaw clenching while he white-knuckled the handle of the shovel. "Don't be ridiculous. I'll help you as soon as I'm finished."

"Now, Pastor Noah," Marv cut in, "this lovely young lady needs some assistance, and seeing as we're not being much help to you, perhaps we could be of service to her." And, like the gentleman he was, he snuck a peek down the front of my blouse as he wrapped an arm around my waist and tugged me into his side.

I worked hard to school my features, making sure the perverted old man currently holding me far too close for my liking didn't notice my flinch. Still, I couldn't stop the slight narrowing of my eyes or the subtle clench of my jaw. Especially when Dirty Old Man's hand got a little low on my back for polite company.

"Marv," Noah said. *Snapped*, really. He took a step closer to us, his eyes locked on me as he spoke to his parishioner. And even though I'd tried as much as I could to keep a poker face to cover my discomfort, it was clear in the way Noah appraised me that he'd seen it. He knew. And he didn't like it. "I'm pretty sure Esther said she wanted to take some mums down to the nursing home once you were finished turning over the flowerbeds here. You might not want to add more projects to your day at this point."

Noah and I had been playing this back-and-forth game for months. I'd worked him up and pissed him off more times than I could count. But in all that time, I'd never once heard him use that tone of voice—with anyone. One that said, *Do not fuck with me*. I didn't even know pastors *had* that tone. And I definitely didn't know I'd be turned on by it.

Marv, as thick as a set of encyclopedias, wasn't picking up what Noah was putting down. He waved a dismissive hand. "She's playing bridge with her friends. An extra half hour won't be any trouble."

Because my eyes were locked on Noah, still mesmerized by the low timbre of his voice, the harsh lines of his clenched jaw—sadly free from stubble, as it was every Sunday—Marv caught me off guard when he tugged me toward him. I stumbled, my heel getting stuck in the crack in the sidewalk. As I tried to right myself and keep from falling—either to the ground or farther into the dirty bastard at my side—Noah jumped toward me. His shovel fell to the ground just as he caught me by the elbow, steadying me.

"Hey," I snapped at Marv, ready to cuss him out—old man or not—because I didn't take well to being jerked around without my consent.

"I'll handle this, Marv." Noah's voice brooked no argument as he pulled me closer to him—and farther away from the Dirty Old Man. Then low enough so only I could hear, he asked, "You okay?"

I couldn't even appreciate the feel of Noah next to me, how nice it felt to be so close, because I was too focused on what he'd said. I'd been manhandled by one guy with his hands and by the other with his words. Wasn't that just my luck?

Marv held up his hands in surrender. "If you wanted to help the pretty lady, Pastor, all you had to do was say so." Then with chuckles from his band of buddies, they all moseyed off, leaving the sidewalk to just Noah and me.

Once they were gone, I spun on him. "You'll *handle* this?" I tugged my elbow free from his hand and crossed my arms over my chest as I leveled a glare in his direction. "You handle your balls, Noah. You do *not* handle a woman."

Normally, if any guy had said that to me, he'd find out exactly how painful a stiletto on his arch was. But with Noah? God, he confused me like no other. *Infuriated* me like no other. Said something completely caveman, followed by concern for my well-being. Who *did* that?

And why the hell was I so turned on by it?

"It's just a turn of phrase," he said, still watching me. Still appraising. "Don't be ridiculous."

"Don't be *ridiculous*? Are you shitting me right now? *You* are the one being ridiculous. All I wanted was some goddamn help moving my goddamn planters and then you—"

"And then I made sure you didn't fall on your ass right there in the middle of the sidewalk." He dropped his gaze, letting his eyes travel over me. From the tips of my high heels, over the silk of my seamed stockings, to the skirt he had no idea I was bare under, and all the way up to the blouse he thought was inappropriate for me to wear. Especially around the dirty old men. Then he bit his bottom lip, his eyes dropping back down to my stocking-encased legs. "I wouldn't want you to run those silky stockings you have on."

My nipples hardened, my pussy growing wet— all because of a slow perusal from a man. No, not just any man… Noah. "You have a problem with my stockings, Pastor No?"

"No problem, though I do wonder how appropriate they are, considering you seem to want to work on the outside of your shop."

I nearly laughed. He thought he could play chicken with me? Call my bluff, and see if I'd break? Little did he know it wasn't in my DNA to back down.

Two steps and I was in his space, breathing in his scent as his heat enveloped me. He swallowed but didn't step back. Feeling emboldened, I lifted a hand and played with his very top button—always buttoned up, always hiding himself. Slowly, I pushed it through the hole, revealing more of his skin than I'd ever seen. A small dusting of dark hair littered his chest, and I *ached* to see more.

"I wasn't exactly planning on doing the work, now was I? And considering I'm not wearing any panties under this skirt, the stockings are the least of my concerns."

chapter three

NOAH

NO ONE HAD ever challenged me the way Harper did. No one had ever made me experience such a wicked flip of emotions. One second, I was enamored of her style and attitude; the next, I was ready to kill her. Right then, standing in front of the church I led and hearing her whisper the word panties, killing felt much closer than it should have.

I stood locked in place for a solid five seconds, staring at the temptress. Unable to fully process what she'd said. Unable to pull my mind away from the image of her with nothing on at all. Nothing covering her… My eyes traveled down of their own accord, staring hard at the tight skirt she wore. Trying to see through it to finally know what was underneath. Would she be bare? Or would she tease her lovers with a thin trail leading to her personal holy land?

Did she have tattoos or piercings? Something about her confidence made me think she might. But where, and what?

I was trapped in those questions, unable to think of anything else. Unable to move. Unable to leave her alone. Until the sound of a car starting up reminded me of where I was, the person the town needed me to be, and how much I wanted not to be him right then.

I needed a five-minute break from being a pastor, and I was going to take it.

"Come with me," I said, tugging Harper along toward the back door of the church.

Harper didn't resist my directions, but she certainly didn't want me to think she was okay with them. "In case it wasn't clear by the fact that I still have on the outfit you told me I should stop wearing, I'm not exactly fond of being told what to do, Pastor No."

And yet, she followed me.

"Spewing anger at me isn't going to help your cause, Miss Davis." I dropped my voice, keeping my words just between us. "There are so many better things you could use that pretty mouth for."

Her arm in my hand went stiff, and I had to issue a gentle reminder to keep moving. But Harper wasn't one to surrender easily. She also had no idea how badly I'd wanted to get her naked or how long those fantasies had haunted me. She'd learn, though. Soon.

But once Harper regained her footing, she didn't acquiesce. Instead, she laughed. Of course. "You're getting awful cocksure for a guy who's in front of his church. You have fantasies of me getting on my knees in the rectory? Yeah, not happening."

"The rectory is the residence, and while I'd love to get you alone in my house, that might be a bad idea for this morning. Besides, I'd prefer you on your knees in the narthex."

Harper stared, gaping, looking completely dumbfounded by my words. Then she shook her head and looked askance. "Still not happening." She tugged her shirt down, the slick, red fabric sliding lower over her full breasts. Exposing more skin. Highlighting what looked like a barbell through each hard nipple. I'd seen those same shadows a hundred times, caught glimpses of shapes that told me she had her nipples pierced. Those hints, those shadows, always made my cock weep with the need to touch. Today was no different.

I was going to rip that damned fabric from her skin if I didn't get a hold of myself. Rip it off and ravish every inch of her, discover every secret, which was exactly what I wanted to do. I wanted to worship her body as a man should worship a woman. Give her every bit of my time and attention, of my efforts, so I could watch her fall apart. We could deal with her being on her knees another time.

Keeping my hand soft on her arm, barely needing to offer any encouragement, to be honest, I pulled her into the back entrance of the church. A long hall with doors on each side greeted us, and I moved with purpose toward the one I knew would give us a few moments alone. The preschool met down this hall during the week, and many of the rooms were used for various educational experiences for them. Toy room, library, music room…all fine. All places I wasn't stopping.

Instead, I picked a door almost all the way down on the right, one I had the key to in my pocket. It had once been an office for someone because there was a desk and a few chairs, but the room hadn't been used in years. In fact, no one ever came down the hall this far except to clean.

We were alone.

The lock turned silently, the door swinging open without a whisper. Good. I directed Harper ahead of me, following her into the room, then closing the door behind me. Before she could react, before she could start again with her angry words, I pushed her back against the wall and caged her in with my body.

"You like to tease me, don't you, Harper?"

That chin rose, her eyes sparking in defiance. "I like to tease everyone. But you *are* exceptionally fun, yes."

"And what if I said I was done being teased?" I leaned closer, letting my lips brush against the shell of her ear. Pressing my hips into hers so she could feel how done I truly was. "What if I said I was calling your bluff?"

Her nipples brushed against my chest as she took a deep, almost shuddering breath. "I'd say I'm going to call *yours*. We're in your church, Noah. Do you expect me to believe you're going to, what? Fuck me over that desk?"

Her sarcastic laugh cut off quickly when I grabbed

her hip and tugged her body against mine. "Maybe next time. Right now, I want to see if you're lying to me about the panties."

Yeah, that refusal to believe I was serious disappeared, and her rueful expression was replaced by something that looked an awful lot like lust. Game on.

I slid my hand down her side, touching for the first time, irritated and intrigued by the texture of her clothes. I wanted skin, yet that blouse—that damned dark red cape waving at me—was so soft and almost shiny. So her. I almost stayed right there, kept my fingers brushing over the silkiness, but I was on a mission. One that meant my hand needed to go lower. Much lower.

Harper inhaled sharply when I ran my hand down her thigh to the edge of her skirt. She also spread her legs a bit. Just enough that I knew she was in this with me. Just enough to give me the green light to let go of Pastor Noah and be plain old Noah for a while.

And plain old Noah wanted to get his hands on Harper's pussy.

"Are you wet, Miss Davis?" I asked as I teased the skin of her thigh at the edge of that skirt. "Your nipples are hard, and your legs are shaking. I bet that pussy's wet for me as well, isn't it?"

She didn't answer. I wasn't even sure she could. Her mouth hung open, those plush lips parting in a way that made me long to slide my cock between them. But I had something else I wanted to do. Something I needed to accomplish first.

I was going to make this woman come.

I tugged at the hem of her skirt, making sure to press my aching cock into her hip. I needed the relief, and she needed a reminder that I was a man, one who wanted her. Who lusted for her. Harper stared up at me, her eyes searching, her breath shuddering as she inhaled. Yeah. I had her attention for sure. I just needed to push her a little more.

"You thought I was a virgin, didn't you?" I asked as I slid my hand back up her thigh, this time underneath her skirt. The edge of the stockings she wore made me groan, the feel of her soft flesh above them almost making me growl. This woman was so sexy, so blatant about her sexuality. It was both a relief and a warning. Women like Harper sometimes used sex as a weapon—I'd seen that enough to know it. But at that point, with my palm against her thigh and my fingers almost to the pussy I sought, I didn't care. Let her try—I'd fight back. And I'd win. Not because I could overpower her, but because I could let her be her. Because I wanted her to stay this wild, untamable thing.

Because I wanted her exactly how she was and had since the very first time I saw her.

"Last chance," I whispered before biting down on her earlobe. She jumped and gasped, trembling through her shock. She also gripped my shoulders tighter and tilted her hips forward. Pulling me closer and seeking more. Perfect.

I slid my fingers up just a little more, nearly collapsing against her as I got my first touch of her pussy. Hot. So hot, and definitely wet. The very tops of her thighs were slick, the lips of her pussy soaked. And she was bare.

My cock nearly exploded at the thought.

"Do you have any idea how many nights I've sat up and wondered what this would feel like?" I slid a single finger inside, circling her, prepping her for more. Closing my eyes for a second at the simple pleasure of feeling her sweet pussy clench. "It's even better than I imagined. You're so soft, so warm. Are you ready for more, doll? Should I stop teasing that pussy?"

Her fingers pressed deep into my flesh as she clutched at me, as she tugged me closer. As she gave way to her need. "If you're gonna do it, *do it*."

Damn, did I love the challenging look she shot me. As if she still didn't think I would cross that line even though I had one finger inside her. As if she had doubts that I'd actually fuck her with my hand, right there and then. She had no idea I'd been dreaming of doing this and more every day for months.

Time to make that dream a reality.

I slipped a second finger inside, stretching her a little. The responding groan, the way she arched her back and rocked her hips into my hand…so fucking sexy. Everything about her was, but this…this pure reaction to what I was doing to her. This wild, unfettered response to my body and my words. This was my heaven. This was my home.

This was everything I had ever wanted.

A couple of shallow thrusts, and then I pressed deep. Harper caught her breath, her eyes closing for a moment as I focused solely on what my hand could do to her. On how much pleasure I knew I could give her. I circled her clit with my thumb, slowly increasing pressure on each pass, and moved my fingers in that come-hither motion to find her most hidden spot. I kept my eyes locked on her face, kept my body pressed tight against her. Watching… waiting. I needed a sign that I'd gotten this right, that I had found what I was seeking. That I could give her as much pleasure—

She jerked, and her eyes popped open on a particularly strong slide deep, deep within her. Bingo.

"That's it, doll. I've got it now, don't I?" I kept curling my fingers, kept pressing in deep to hit that spot, not giving her a second to retreat from what I knew was building inside her. Pushing her closer to the edge she needed to jump off. Her eyes stayed on mine, wide and unfocused, her mouth hanging open as she moaned and gasped. As her body worked in tandem with mine.

Her head fell back, and those beautiful eyes closed as the rest of her body opened for me. "Fuck, Noah."

The walls of her body clenched and released in a slow rhythm, and the sounds coming from where my hand worked had become obscene. So wet, so swollen for me. She had to be almost there. I could feel the tension building in her body, could hear how her breaths had sped up.

"Harder." She gasped, clinging to my shoulders with an almost painful hold. "Fuck…I need…faster." Oh hell, her demands were so fucking hot. Harper kept riding my hand, taking what she needed, refusing to be a simple participant. That was hot, too. Almost too hot for me to deal with. I pressed my aching cock into her hip and growled through the need to rock. The need to sink deep. The need to come all over her. This wasn't my moment; it was hers. She'd pushed and pushed and pushed me, and I'd finally broken. I'd get my pleasure when she did the same.

My doll surprised me, though. She rocked and groaned and hissed and cursed, just as I'd expected. But she also moaned long and loud before grabbing my face and tugging me down to her. And then she kissed the hell out of me. It wasn't the first kiss I'd once thought we'd share, wasn't sweet or tentative. This was rough and brutal—all teeth and tongue and battle. A fight to dominate and lead. It was hot. Fucking hot. Too fucking hot.

"You're going to make me come like a schoolboy if you keep kissing me like that," I said when I finally pulled myself from her mouth.

Her lips turned up in an arrogant sort of smirk. "Not sure I see the problem with that."

I leaned in, pressing my lips to hers once more. Sweeter this time. Softer. Giving her a moment to think she had me before I went in for the kill.

"I'd much rather come in that pretty mouth of yours, but not yet. I want to feel you come on my hand first." Before I could enjoy her reaction, before I could do more than lean her back a little and work a third finger inside her, the back door slammed closed.

"What's that?" Harper asked, only slightly more

focused. Her hips still rocked against my hand, her body still quivering with every thrust. I couldn't stop.

"Shh." I pressed a soft kiss to her lips, leaning closer so I could force her legs to spread wider, so I could whisper in her ear as well. "Someone's in the hall."

Harper's entire body went stiff. "Did you lock the door?"

I pushed her knees farther apart with my own, opening her even more, speeding up the thrusts of my hand. I could see the warring emotions on her face, could almost sense them. The fear of getting caught, the excitement of almost getting caught. The arousal of knowing we could get caught if we weren't quiet. Fuck, there was no way I was letting her get away from me now.

"I don't remember." I ran my nose along her neck, enjoying the way she trembled at my lie. How she was back to fucking my hand with her greedy pussy. "Does it matter?"

She pulled away, looking me right in the eye as she whispered, "Someone could walk in."

Footsteps in the hall grew closer, but Harper didn't stop, so neither did I. We locked gazes, both silent other than the sucking sound of her pussy taking my fingers. Other than the breaths we simply couldn't hold. Her knee trembled against my hip, and her arm shook where she had it locked around my neck. Obscene, that image was. My hand between her legs, my fingers buried inside her as she spread herself around me. Obscene and perfect. Something no one else would ever see.

"Answer me," I whispered just as the footsteps stopped outside the room we were in. "Does it matter? Do you care that they might think the local sex shop owner sullied their sweet pastor? That sin is winning over salvation right now?"

My words were more breath than anything, my eyes boring into hers. She paused, her pussy clenching hard on my fingers just before she shook her head slowly. Decidedly.

Perfectly.

I leaned in and bit her lip as I sped up my hand, as I pressed my thumb hard against her clit and worked her pussy in earnest. She gasped and rocked, not even pulling away from me as the handle jiggled, as someone checked to see if the door was locked or not. She didn't care if they got in, and neither did I. Though I was glad I'd remembered to actually lock the fucking thing. No way was I stopping. No way was I giving up the feel of her pussy soaking my hand. I wanted to make her come, needed it, and no one was going to keep me from that moment.

The rattling of the handle stopped, the footsteps retreating back down the hall, but it didn't matter. Nothing mattered but my hand and Harper's wet, swollen pussy.

"I know you want to be loud," I said just as I flicked my thumb over her clit and pressed hard on that spot inside her. Her pussy clenched once around my fingers, locking tight as she trembled. I didn't let up, though. I pushed deeper, moved my fingers faster, and pressed down hard on her clit.

"Let me hear you, doll. Let me know how good I make you feel."

Harper came with a squeal that probably could have been heard in the chapel, that could likely bring back whoever had been in the hall, though I didn't care. I was too focused on how beautiful she was in that moment. How completely unrestrained and free. How fucking out of control.

"That's it, doll. Come for me. Can't wait to feel this on my cock. Though, I think I'd prefer it on my tongue first." I worked her through her orgasm, massaging her clit and pussy until the clenches tapered off. Until she practically collapsed against me. "What do you think? Should I eat you before I fuck you? Would you ride my face like you just rode my hand?"

She groaned and dropped her head to my shoulder, mumbling something under her breath. I pulled my fingers from inside her, cupping her still, not ready to give up the access she'd gifted me. Wishing I could slide deep inside her right then and fuck her until I got to feel that hot, tight heaven come on my cock.

But that wasn't in the cards right then.

Rucked up, sexed up, sated, and not-quite-coherent, Harper whimpered and rolled herself against my palm. "Why are you stopping?"

"Should I keep going?" I slid a finger against her clit, grinning when she shivered at the touch.

"I was more worried about you." She ran her hand along my cock, making me groan at the thought of all the things I wanted her to do to it. But not yet. Not today. I had plans, and they were going to take a little bit more time.

I grabbed her hand, pressing it harder against where I was so aching for her, before bringing a finger from my other hand to my lips. It was still wet from her, still smelled like her. As she watched, I pushed the finger into my mouth. Sweet and salty, the taste of her exploded on my tongue just as I'd known it would. It was everything I'd imagined and more, everything I'd dreamed of when I pictured her laid out before me with her legs spread and my face between her thighs. I practically groaned.

When I slid the finger back through my lips, I leaned close once more. Letting her feel how hard I was for her. Letting her smell herself on my breath as I whispered, "I want to have you for dessert before I fuck you, but that means I need to take you to dinner first."

She blinked, her entire body stiffening as I watched, and then she pushed me away. Her emotional shield slid down once more, her eyes going flat and her body closing to me. Fuck, that obviously wasn't what she was ready for. My Harper—the one who'd challenged me to make her come, the one who'd fucked my hand while kissing me with such passion—was gone. The woman straightening her clothes and patting her hair into place was closed off, uninterested, and done.

"Thanks for the offer, but dinner isn't an option. I need to get back to the store." She pushed me away, heading for the door without even looking my way.

The fabric of her skirt tugged taut across her ass, her hips swinging. All attitude again. Her denial of us was expected and totally dismissible. I'd caught her off guard when I'd taken charge, and Harper Davis didn't seem to like giving up control. She'd learn, though. Soon enough, she'd figure out how to deal with me when I was the one leading us.

Soon enough, she'd be mine. I'd make damn sure of it.

chapter four

I COULDN'T GET out of the church fast enough. I didn't pay attention to see if anyone was around before I pushed through the back door and hurried around the side of the building and across the street, straight to the shop. With a distracted wave to Chris and Genesis, who'd arrived in the time I'd been gone, I escaped into my office, shut the door, and collapsed into my chair.

Holy shit, what had just happened? I mean… *Holy. Shit.* Had Noah actually just fingered me in the same building he gave the Sunday sermon? Had I actually *let* him?

For months, we'd been circling each other—me teasing him until he'd snap and storm off, leaving me utterly pleased with myself, then we'd rinse and repeat. We had a good thing going. Easy. Predictable.

Except this time, he'd turned that predictability on its head. This time, he *hadn't* stalked off. This time… he'd teased back.

Hadn't been much teasing in what he'd done, though.

I closed my eyes, transporting myself back to that darkened office, stale with nonuse. He'd been firm and hard against me, and if I hadn't had the wall against my back, I wasn't so sure I'd have been able to support myself. Not when his words had met my ear. Not when he'd groaned low and deep as he'd touched my pussy for the first time. And jesus*fuck* had he touched it. I'd just had the hottest orgasm of my entire life— and I'd had the privilege of having some spectacular orgasms in my years—by a man who I'd assumed was a caged lion.

Turned out he wasn't so caged, after all.

And not only was he not caged, he was apparently ready and willing to do dirty, dirty things to me.

I sucked in a breath, my exhale shuddering through my lips as I dropped my head into my hands. That was fine, right? No big deal. It wasn't like Noah was any different from any other guy I'd been with, barring the major exception—that he spent his days in a church instead of an office.

No big deal.

Weird, turned out repeating it over and over to yourself didn't actually make it a reality. I was afraid no big deal was actually a very big deal.

What I needed right now was definitely not to be alone. I needed someone who could give it to me straight. Someone who would tell me how fucking crazy this was and tell me to get my mind out of the land of amazing orgasms and forget about a hookup with the pastor.

A hookup. With the *pastor*.

Well, at least Grandma would be happy because I'd definitely come closer to Jesus.

Once I made it out into the front section of the store, Chris had already gone home for the day, and Gen was busy straightening a new display of glass dildos.

"My God, these look fantastic, don't they? I'm definitely buying one of these bad boys tonight. Brandon will flip when I bring it—" She straightened as soon as she looked at me over her shoulder. "What's with the face?"

"I just did something I probably shouldn't have."

She looked me up and down, a smirk drawing her lips to the side. "Well, if that something was get laid—because you definitely have that Just Got Laid glow about you—then I say, *lies*. You *should*. Always."

"Not laid. Not exactly."

With a grin, Gen left the display to settle into a chair at the front and gestured for me to take the seat across from her. Fitting, really, that I'd discuss this, even vaguely, while sitting on the furniture left from my grandmother.

"I can work with 'not exactly.'" Gen clasped her hands together and leaned toward me once I sat down. "Tell me everything."

Everything? No, I definitely couldn't do that. It

wasn't every day someone got fingered by the pastor, and I was sure Noah would want a little discretion. He'd said he was going to take me to dinner this week, but I assumed that was code for swing by my place after dark, slip in and slip out without anyone the wiser. He had his career to worry about—his whole life, really. Being a pastor wasn't like being an accountant. It wasn't just a job. It was a lifestyle…a commitment. That was something I couldn't wrap my head around. I could barely commit to a hairstylist.

Besides *his* life, this situation wouldn't exactly bode well for my already meager reputation. Not if I was caught sullying Temperance Falls' favorite pastor.

"I did something," I said.

"Yeah, I figured that much." Gen rolled her eyes. "Get to the part with the orgasms."

So grateful for a moment of levity after all these confusing emotions swarming around in my head, I laughed. "I will, but I need to talk this out first."

"Here for it. Now spill."

"There's this guy. We've sort of been…circling each other. For months."

"Months, huh? That's some serious foreplay."

That was the damn truth. *Explosive* foreplay. Could that have been why the orgasm had been so powerful? That and the fact that it was so…forbidden? I'd gotten off in some pretty risqué places, but never a church. That was taboo even for me.

I nodded. "I've always assumed he was sort of off-limits, so it was like playing without any of the consequences, you know?"

"Is he married?" Gen held up her hands before I could respond. "No judging from me, just trying to get a feel for the sitch."

"No, no, nothing like that. His…job wouldn't really take kindly to him being with me."

"Because of Sin? Well, that's some bullshit."

Sin was what it was, all right. And it had nothing to do with my shop.

"Anyway, today he proved something between us wasn't quite as off-limits as I thought it was. I pushed his buttons like always, but this time…"

Gen leaned closer to me, her eyes bright. "Yeah?"

"It was like he snapped. He took me into the place he worked and gave me the most intense orgasm of my life."

"Holy shit…he fucked you at his work even with the whole"—she waved a hand around—"situation?"

"Not fucked, no. Fingered."

"He *fingered* you to your most intense orgasm? Whoa. Those are some magic fingers."

"I know, right? If you're not fingering with your tongue, you're doing it wrong. But holy shit did this guy do it right." I shifted in my seat, remembering his words, the feel of his fingers stretching me, his thumb insistent on my clit as he worked me up and pushed me right over the edge without hesitation.

And then to watch him suck my come right off those fingers? Holy shit.

"Well, it's obvious you need to fuck him. Immediately."

I laughed, propping an elbow on the table

and resting my chin in my hand. "But what about everything else?"

Gen shrugged. "Who cares? If he's not worried about his job—and since he fingered you in his office or wherever, I'm guessing he gives zero fucks about it—then you shouldn't be either."

I didn't say this out loud, but that was only one part of my worries. I'd spent my life on Temperance Falls being called every name in the book. Hussy. Slut. Whore. Easy. Loose. They were titles I'd been born into, thanks to my mom who had me at the ripe old age of fifteen. From that day on, we'd both had a scarlet letter branded on us. My grandmother had done everything she could to steer us both toward the straight and narrow. But my mother was as free with her love as my grandma was frugal. And I'd never really had any interest in living my life for anyone but myself.

So then, why did what the townspeople thought of Noah and me bother me so much?

"This convo is gonna have to wait," Gen said. "The blue-hairs must've been bitching to Pastor No again, because he's on his way over here now."

"He's what?" I snapped my head to look out the window, and sure enough, there he was, strolling across the street like he had no cares in the world. In fact, there was a…smile on his face. And those two buttons I'd undone still sat open, giving the world a first-time glimpse of his chest. A chest I definitely wanted to see in all its glory.

"What the hell got into him? He's *smiling*." Gen

pressed her face closer to the window as she peered outside. "He never smiles when he comes over here. And what the fuck is going on with his shirt? Pastor No has chest hair!"

I didn't have time to tell her I'd been just as surprised as she was because suddenly the front door opened, the bell ringing softly to announce his arrival, and there he stood. In Sin, looking, well, sinful. Somehow his eyes found me almost immediately. And then…then his smile grew.

"Oh my God," Gen whispered. "*Pastor No?*"

"Good afternoon, Miss McKay." He nodded at her, then looked to me, his eyes darkening, his smile turning a bit devious. God, I hoped I was the only one who noticed. "Harper."

"You let Pastor No finger you?" Gen hissed at me.

So much for that hope.

Figuring my best course of action was to ignore her entirely, I stood from the chair and smoothed my skirt. "Pastor Noah. What can we help you with? Something not up to standard for the old biddies?"

"No, nothing like that. In fact, I'm free from church responsibilities until Tuesday morning's silent reflection hour." His smile dimmed as he ran his hand down the buttons on his shirt and straightened his shoulders, almost as if he was psyching himself up for something. "I was coming to see if you'd care to join me for dinner tomorrow, Harper. I mentioned it earlier, but I wasn't sure if you remembered."

I blinked. Swallowed. Blinked again. "Say what now?"

"Dinner. With me. I'd like to take you on a date."

I whipped my head around to Gen, who had her chin resting in her hand, obviously enjoying every second of this, then back to Noah. "But...I thought..." I shook my head, because none of this was making any sense. Why was he here? Was he really asking me out on a date? And was he seriously doing it in front of an audience? "Dinner...like, out? At a restaurant?"

"That's usually what a date entails, yes."

"You do know Gen can hear you, right?"

He furrowed his brow. "Is there a reason she shouldn't hear this?"

Um, yeah. Like the fact that she could tell just about anyone what was going on. Or maybe that his whole career was at stake here. What in the actual fuck was going on?

"I just...didn't anticipate you being so open about this. When you said dinner, I assumed you meant..." I trailed off with a shrug.

He went brows up and gave me a flirty smile. "Netflix and chill?"

Gen snorted at the same time a surprised laugh flew from my mouth. "Pretty much."

"While I would never turn down such an invitation, my intentions for tomorrow evening were a little more...public. Like dinner at Nonno Pino's and conversation."

Dinner and conversation. What the hell? I glanced at Gen, who was absolutely no help. She fluttered her fingers at me, before waggling her eyebrows and giving me a thumbs-up. Yeah, super subtle, Gen. Awesome job.

I glanced back at Noah, who was staring intently at me. He was just a guy asking for a date. I'd been out on plenty of dates, and they hadn't meant anything. This was the same. The only reason it had to be different from past situations was if I made it so. And I didn't have to make it so, right? No big deal. I nearly cringed because there was that phrase again. Instead, I swallowed and decided what the hell.

"Dinner. Out." I offered a smile. "What time?"

"I made a reservation for seven. I'll pick you up." Noah leaned in, his fingers brushing against the back of my arm as he pressed a small kiss on my cheek, the innocent touch making my nipples go tight. Then he moved his lips to my ear, his voice dropping low. "Feel free to leave the panties off again."

chapter five

NOAH

THE FOLLOWING NIGHT, I practically bounded up the back stairs leading to Harper's apartment over her shop. Date time—dinner and conversation, getting to know each other, and perhaps a little flirting that could possibly lead to more than flirting. I wasn't focused on that, though. This was our first date, after all.

I'd spent the past twenty-four hours psyching myself up to deal with this date. For as outwardly sexual as my Harper was, she still deserved to be treated like a lady. That meant I would follow her lead on how fast our physical relationship would go. Yesterday could have been a fluke—could have been a single moment of weakness. She could be regretting it.

God, I hoped she wasn't regretting it.

Still, I had to keep my desire for her in check.

Restraint was the word of the night, a fact I reminded my cock of multiple times. I could not fail.

I knocked three times, then glanced down at the street where a couple was walking by hand in hand. That could be Harper and me later. Yes, hand-holding. I liked hand-holding. That'd be the perfect end to our date. A stroll along the waterfront with her hand in mine. I should remind her to bring a coat since it could get cold later.

The snick of the door opening had me turning back around, smiling. Ready to greet her as a gentleman should. But the vision before me kicked the gentleman back down the stairs and left nothing behind but a seething, whirling ball of testosterone and sexual desire.

"Hi, Noah. I was just finishing up."

I couldn't move, couldn't breathe. Harper stood in her open doorway wearing a short skirt that moved when she did. What she wasn't wearing was a blouse. Harper had answered her door in only a skirt and a lacy purple bra, the jewelry through her nipples a beacon for my eyes. Barbells…I knew it. Between the skin on display and the way her breasts seemed ready to spill over the fabric at any moment, I was mesmerized. Stunning was an understatement.

Her lips—all thick and red and perfect for wrapping around my cock—quirked up into a half smile. "Are you planning on coming inside, or are you going to stand there and stare? I'm starting to get a complex." She spun and walked back inside her apartment. That skirt—that evil little piece of fabric—practically danced around her thighs as she walked. It also rose with each step just enough for me to see the tops of the fucking stockings a lot like what she'd worn yesterday.

Come inside? Yes. Immediately.

I followed her inside, but that skirt obliterated any sort of plans I had for resisting her. I grabbed her hand and spun her around, pressing her back to the wall. Settling us in the patch of sunlight from the window of her hallway as the door swung closed behind us. We were alone. The quiet of her apartment made that small hallway feel closer, made the space seem more intimate. Made the outside world disappear. The scent of lilacs only intensified that sensation. I was surrounded by her, every sense overtaken. Every inch of me hers.

Perfect.

"After the performance in church yesterday, I'd assumed you'd seen a girl in her bra before." Her dark eyebrow quirked up...another challenge. "Was I wrong?"

"You're not just any girl, though, are you?" I couldn't hold back the slight smirk as her eyes widened. Score one for the pastor. "There's nothing more I want than to strip that fabric from your body so I can see"—I ran a finger over the side of her breast, skirting right at the edge of the jewelry through her nipple, before dropping my hand back to her hip—"everything you have to show me. But this is our first date. I'm trying to be a gentleman."

The way I squeezed her, pulling her body against

mine so I could press my rock-hard cock against her stomach—the way I couldn't stop staring at her—belied my words. My restraint was wavering, my control shredding. And by the way she looked up at me with fire in her eyes, she knew it.

"You weren't a gentleman yesterday when you stuck your hand up my skirt."

I leaned in, dropping soft kisses along her neck. Unable not to steal a taste of her to join in the rest of my senses. She tasted like she smelled, and the dichotomy of such an innocent scent on such a brazen woman wasn't lost on me. Pure sin. "If I remember right, you didn't seem to mind my hand up your skirt."

She grabbed my belt loops and tugged, rocking her hips into my cock. "No, I didn't."

Oh, hell. My hands shook as I fought to keep them from sliding under clothes and seeking soft, warm skin. A fight I was quickly losing.

"And is that what you want? You want me to come inside and make you come on my cock?" I ran my fingers over the edge of her garter belt where it lay across her ass, slipping my fingers underneath the edge of it only to find skin. No panties again. Fuck, this woman was perfect for me. So soft. So fucking silky and warm. I grabbed her bare ass with both hands, kneading her flesh. Groaning at the feel of her skin against mine.

She rose to the balls of her feet, pressing harder against my aching cock, and brushed her lips against my ear as she whispered, "As you seem to have figured out, I'm not wearing panties and wasn't planning on it for this so-called date. I thought I was being fairly obvious, Pastor No."

Restraint—shattered.

"Turn around, Harper."

The little vixen gave me a solid stare, even going so far as to raise an eyebrow at me. I knew I was pushing her—Harper definitely wasn't one to take orders—but I couldn't help myself. I had to have her. Finally, she turned, rubbing her ass against my cock in a way that sent lightning bolts along my spine. This woman was pushing me hard, and I loved every second of it. I let her put space between us, let her have a single moment where she could hold on to that fantasy of Pastor No.

I wasn't saying no tonight.

Harper shot me a saucy sort of smile over her shoulder, her hands against the wall. Her ass popped out. "Can I assume you don't want a glass of wine? I set out a bottle and everything…"

But my chain had been pulled too tight for her sass. I pushed her against the wall, covering her body with mine as I pressed my hips into her ass. Desperate and needy for her.

"I have no interest in wine, and my guess is you already knew that," I said just before I bit down on her neck. She jerked and gasped, spreading her legs when I nudged my thigh between them. "Do you want wine, Harper? Do you want me to keep being the gentleman who wants to take you to dinner? The nice guy who says the right things and behaves himself while pouring you a glass of good Chardonnay? Or do you want me to fuck you right up against this wall?"

"Goddamn," she said, reaching back to grab my hip. "Where the hell did you come from?"

"Pennsylvania. Now spread those legs a little more, doll. I'm going to need some room to work."

She inched her feet apart, bending slightly in invitation. I flipped that slip of a skirt up and over her hips, finally getting a view of exactly what I wanted. Ass on display, pussy peeking out at me, she was a vision of every want and fantasy I'd ever had. That soft skin was too much to ignore, the temptation too much to resist. I ran my hand up and down the length of her, teasing her pussy with my knuckles, watching as her thighs flexed with every pass.

But I wasn't all about her pussy. No, sir. There was something hidden beneath the lace of her bra. Something I'd seen shadows of. Something I needed to get my hands on. I moved one hand around the front of her, grabbing her breast. Kneading it. Sighing as I felt the hard ridge of jewelry there.

"You have pierced nipples."

I could almost hear the laugh in her voice as she said, "Excellent deductive skills, Noah."

But I knew how to handle the sarcastic side of her. I slipped my hand inside the flimsy fabric of her bra, pinching the metal barbell between my fingers and thumb. Tweaking it. Tugging it. Harper moaned and twitched with each pull, telling me exactly how sensitive those bars of steel made her nipples. Giving me ideas on what to do once I got my mouth on her.

"I've seen the shadows beneath your shirts a hundred times and wondered." I gave the barbell one last tug before placing my hand against the wall, supporting myself as I once again stroked over her pussy. "I'll have fun with those later."

"I sure hope so. Just so you know, they respond well to tongues."

Always brash, my Harper. Always so forward. I loved it. But still, I needed to check in with her. Had to know.

"Are you sure about this?" I asked as I leaned in to nibble down her neck again. "I'll stop if you don't want me—"

"Do I look like I'm having second thoughts?" Again, she spread her legs, her ass shaking a little as she did.

Done. In seconds, I had my pants unfastened and pushed down to my knees, one of the condoms I'd stored in my wallet as a just-in-case clenched tight in my fist. Just in case had just become right the fuck now, and I was thankful I'd thought to be prepared. I tore open the packet with my teeth, looking forward to the day when she trusted me enough to go in without it. Oh fuck. Bare. Someday, I'd slide into that sweet pussy bare—something I'd never done in my life. Something that made the deepest, darkest, most testosterone-filled corners of my brain stand up and cheer. She was going to have me dripping out of her one day. Not today, but soon. Fuck, that thought was hot.

Once I'd sheathed my cock, I gripped the base, sliding the tip through her wetness. Preparing.

Fighting with my internal teenager not to just slam inside and bunny-fuck her until I came. I had to get her off, had to feel her clenching around me. This was going to be quick, but it needed to be good for her.

"I have to tell you," I said as I started to push inside. I caught my breath and held still, unable to speak. Unable to move. She felt too good—too warm and wet and hot in all the right ways. Soft yet tight, her pussy enveloped my cock. One flinch, and I was going to come. I couldn't yet—not until she got hers at least once. I just needed a moment to breathe first.

"What?" she asked, turning around to look at me over her shoulder. "Noah?"

I couldn't resist her. I leaned in to kiss those sultry lips. Softly. Sweetly. "It's been a while, Harper. I'm not sure how long…"

My words were cut off with my groan as she pushed back away from the wall, forcing me deeper. Fucking herself with my cock as I held still. Good Lord, this woman was going to kill me.

"I trust that even if you go off in three seconds, you'll still make sure I come. Am I wrong?"

"No," I gasped, growling as my legs began to shake. "You're not wrong. I want to make you come so bad. It's all I need right now."

"So do it."

I nodded, pushing deeper. Fuck, she was so hot. So wet. Her pussy grasped me so right. There was no way I was going to last. I dropped my hand between her legs, sliding my thumb back and forth between her lips until I found her clit. She gasped and jerked when I pressed down, when I teased that sensitive flesh. The smell of lilacs seemed to increase as our bodies moved, as we writhed against one another right there in her hallway. I hadn't even taken her on the couch or the bed, hadn't given her a chance for either of us to get naked. Not that I thought she cared. Her pussy tightened around me, spasming slightly as I pushed her further. As I teased her clit and thrust deep. She liked this…liked the roughness and the spontaneity. Fucking perfect.

"That's it, doll. Let go. Let me feel you come." I circled her clit while she grasped at the wall and cursed. Her body was tight, her muscles ready. On another hard thrust, she slammed her hand down. It didn't hit the wall this time but the window. The one looking out across the street. Framing the church almost perfectly. A little slice of the pastor side of me peeking into the moment, something that only made things that much hotter.

"Noah." Harper leaned forward, her hand covering the small window, pushing her ass back against me in ways that should have been illegal.

Fuck, I was going to come, but I needed her to go first. Needed to feel it. To hear her cries and feel her arousal drip down between us. I wouldn't leave her wanting. Ever. I pumped harder, quicker. Worked my thumb with more pressure. I wanted to close my eyes, to fall into the sensation and let go, but I couldn't look away from Harper. She was so beautiful like this, so honest and raw as she worked her body with mine. And needy—fuck, was she needy. Just a few more. Just a little.

Her pussy clenched on my cock a second before she moaned in that keening way I already knew meant she was coming. I slid deeper, overpowering her, making sure she got as much out of this as she could. Pushing myself right to that edge as well. I came with a groan, my face buried in her neck, my chest heaving as I tried—and failed—to catch my breath. Perfection. Every second, every sensation, was fucking perfection.

But as the caveman retreated and the gentleman I'd been raised to be came back, something akin to guilt began to make my gut tense. I'd fucked her like an animal against her wall. This was supposed to be our first date, and I'd fucked it up. Literally.

"C'mon, doll," I said as I slid out of her. Harper twitched and sighed, but she didn't move. That was fine. I grabbed her around the shoulders and under the knees and hoisted her into my arms.

"Where are we going?"

"I'm going to clean us both up, then you're going to finish getting dressed." It didn't take me long to find her bathroom. Bright and open, the space had an airiness to it that fit the woman who lived there, but I was too far into mission mode to stop and look around.

"For what?" Harper asked, her voice sharp. Her shock evident.

I set her on the bathroom counter and grabbed a small towel from the shelf by the tub, stopping only to rid myself of the latex that had been between us. "Dinner."

Her surprise only made me feel worse. Mouth open, eyes wide, she sat there as I wet the towel and spread her legs. It wasn't until I had finished cleaning her up that she finally remembered how to speak.

"You're still taking me to dinner?"

I kept my eyes on hers as I wiped off my cock then tossed the towel into the basket by the door. Once clean, I leaned in, caging her on the counter with a hand on either hip. Her eyes were huge as they stared into mine, her wariness obvious. She still smelled like flowers, though, which had suddenly become a huge turn-on. One I couldn't resist.

My lips met hers in a fiery, powerful kiss that left her breathless. I cradled her face in my hands, unable not to touch, unwilling to let her go. Forehead pressed against hers, I took a moment to simply be in her space, and then I answered her ridiculous question.

"Yes. I'm taking you to dinner. We *will* have the first date I promised you. Then I'm bringing you back home and walking you to your door, and you can either send me on my way or I can come back in here and fuck you until you can't walk tomorrow. The choice is yours, but whether you let me into your bed or not, I'm going to take you out. Like a fucking gentleman should."

chapter six

WHERE THE HELL had Noah Reid come from? What kind of guy came in, fucked a girl, and *then* took her out to dinner? Certainly none I'd ever gone out with. I was sure it was because Noah was just hungry and felt like an ass for being…*greedy* with me. And really, there was no other word to describe it. Not with the way he'd clutched my hips. How he'd leaned into me. How he'd inhaled my scent as if it were the only kind of sustenance he needed.

I glanced over at him as he kept pace with me, a serene smile on his face. Waving at people walking past as if everything were totally normal. As if it were an everyday occurrence that he was strolling around, holding hands with the owner of the local sex toy shop. As if he hadn't just fucked me within an inch of my life against the wall next to a window with a view of his church.

Holy *hell*. The way he'd been eager but almost hesitant, like he'd wanted to gorge himself on a feast while still savoring every bite, had nearly been my undoing. Jesus, if he could fuck like that after being celibate for years, what would he be able to do in a week? In a *month*?

Then again, it didn't matter what he'd be able to do in that time frame, because it wouldn't be with me. I didn't do relationships, full stop. And Noah was a relationship man—it was written all over him.

The walk to the restaurant took hardly any time, but it felt like a lifetime. So many looks, double takes, and hushed commentary from our fellow Temperance Falls residents out enjoying the nice fall evening. I wasn't a stranger to the gossip mill, but this was different. This affected more than just me.

Once inside Nonno Pino's, the hostess led us to our table, and Noah pulled out my chair for me before taking a seat for himself. And then we were alone—or as alone as we could be in a dining room full of people, all sneaking not-so-covert looks our way.

"You okay over there?" Noah asked. "You're awfully quiet."

"Hmm?" I glanced at him, finding his focus completely on me. Either he was oblivious to what was going on around us, or it didn't bother him. "Yeah, I'm fine. Just…looking at my options." I held up the menu I hadn't even opened yet. Smooth, Harper. Real smooth.

His gaze was sharp, his eyes studying, assessing. I'd spent most of my life letting people see only what I wanted them to, and then Noah blew into it and stripped everything away. Somehow, I showed him way more than I intended to. Way more than I was entirely comfortable with.

Reaching across the table, he grabbed my hand and held it in his, his thumb tracing soft circles on my palm. "Harper. Talk to me."

I blew out a breath and then pointedly looked around, tilting my head toward all the looky-loos. "Aren't you at all worried about people seeing us together?"

He laughed under his breath, his thumb still hypnotizing me with its caresses. "Why would I be? We're just out on a date."

My eyebrows hit my hairline. "I'm the owner of an adult toy shop, Noah. I'm pretty sure there's not a soul on this island who thinks we're *just* dating."

"Well, we're not just dating, are we? We're more than dating, and I'm still allowed to do that."

"You're allowed to date a nice, sweet girl who bakes muffins on Sundays and sings in the church choir. I'm not that girl. The only thing I do religiously on Sundays is run my dildos through the dishwasher."

He gripped my hand tighter and placed his elbows on the table so he could lean closer to me. "I'm allowed to date whomever I like, and that happens to be you. As for the dildos, I'm sure I could help you out with that, so long as it doesn't interfere with Bible study." The side of his mouth kicked up a notch, mischief shining through his eyes. Mischief and lust.

I breathed out a surprised laugh, shaking my head. "So you're telling me it doesn't bother you at all that Donna over there is whispering to her husband about the fact that we're out to dinner right now? And that by tomorrow's silent reflection hour at the church, it's already going to have spread through your congregation like gonorrhea? You're going to have a lot of questions to answer." I glanced at Donna, who was still staring, and fluttered my fingers at her in a wave. She finally spun around, pretending she hadn't been gawking. "Seems like a lot of work for what's going on here."

Noah was quiet for so long, I finally turned my attention back to him. His gaze was on me, the space between his eyebrows pinched, like he couldn't quite figure out the answer to the equation I'd just placed in front of him. Finally, he said, "Questions, I can handle. People talking about us, I can handle. And I'm willing to put in as much work as necessary to get you to see we're great together." He leaned even farther across the table, his voice dropping to a low, sultry tone meant for only my ears. "Harper, I'm a pastor, not a priest. I'm allowed to date, and I'm allowed to choose whomever I want to share my life with. I'm also allowed to fuck you six ways from Sunday so long as it's consensual. What are you so worried about?"

What *was* I so worried about? I'd never once cared

about what hooking up with my previous sexual partners might or might not do to their careers or lives. So why was this different for me? Why was *he* different for me?

Rather than open that can of worms, I shrugged. "I'm already known as the hussy who turned her grandmother's precious Christian bookstore into a den of sin. Now I'm going to be known as the hussy who turned the lovable, *virgin* pastor into a sex fiend." I shot him a wry look. "And don't tell me people don't think you're a virgin…you put out that vibe." Then under my breath, I mumbled, "Or you used to, anyway."

He sat back, grinning, looking altogether too cocky. "Are you trying to tell me you think you've broken my pastorness?"

"You just fucked me up against a wall, *Pastor*, so I'd say it's officially broken."

"I think fingering you in the church offices would have been more damaging to my pastorness, yet I still went and taught Bible study and counseled some of our senior members afterward. Pastor title and aura fully in place." He leaned in again, cupping my hand in both of his. Running his fingers over it. He traced patterns across the palm and back, down my fingers, to my wrist… It was the most innocent erotic touch I'd ever experienced. "My faith is about love and hope, about finding joy in every moment you can. You bring me joy, Harper Davis. Anyone who can't see that or thinks it's wrong simply because of your career isn't the kind of person who would listen to one of my sermons anyway."

I could only stare at him, mouth agape. And he let me, not saying a word as he continued brushing circles over my hand. Who the hell was this guy? When we'd started our combustible flirting all those months ago, I certainly hadn't anticipated ending up here. And yet there we were, half an hour post orgasms, about to have a nice, romantic meal in a public restaurant. No hiding. No secrets. No shame.

"Pastor Noah, I thought that was you."

The interruption startled both of us, but Noah recovered quicker than I did. "Janet, hello. How are you this evening?" he asked, making no move to release my hand. Instead, he continued his mind-numbing caresses as he held a conversation as if this were perfectly normal.

"I'm fine." She slid her eyes to me, then quickly back to Noah when she caught me watching her.

"I believe you know Harper Davis," he said. "She owns the retail establishment across the street from the church."

Her cheeks turned bright red at the mention of the shop. Probably because she was worried I'd rat her out to her pastor. The complimentary mail service I offered at Sin—because in a small-town atmosphere like Temperance Falls, people liked the guise of propriety—had been her best friend since I'd opened the shop. Her latest order had been a thin, silicone dildo, meant for intro to anal play. Something I was quite certain she didn't want her dear pastor knowing about.

Clearing her throat, she nodded at me. "Sure, sure.

Hi, Harper. I didn't expect to see you two together. Just discussing business?"

"Not at all." Noah smiled—not at her, but at me—then gave a wink before looking back in her direction. "Miss Davis and I are dating."

Janet's eyes bulged, her jaw hanging open. "*Dating*? You"—she pointed to Noah—"and…her?" She gestured to me.

Not very subtle, Janet. Though from the way she wasn't at all covert about eye-fucking Noah, it was pretty clear she thought I was encroaching on her territory. I looked her up and down, taking in every inch of her. From her pin-straight and perfectly in-place hair, to the pearl earrings she wore, to her cute little sweater set and pressed slacks, she would've been perfectly at home in the dictionary next to the title: Pastor's Wife.

With a nod, Noah answered her rude-ass question. "Yes, she and I." He turned his body slightly, seemingly giving her all of his attention, save for my hand still held in his. "How's your sister been feeling? I've been praying for her since the surgery."

"Oh, you're just the sweetest," she gushed, placing a hand on his shoulder as she leaned closer to him.

I narrowed my eyes, grinding my teeth together. I didn't have any kind of claim on Noah, but that shit just wasn't cool. You didn't encroach on another girl's date and paw all over him. Never mind the way it made my stomach twist, my hand clenching into a fist between his.

I had to give credit to Noah, though, smooth

motherfucker that he was. He shifted just enough so Janet had no choice but to drop her hand or risk looking like an idiot. While he kept her talking about her sister, he caressed my hand, getting me to unclench my fist. With ease, he deflected her attention from what was going on between us.

And what the hell *was* going on? Months and months we'd had of that delicious back-and-forth, a year's worth of taunting. Delayed gratification. And then in the span of two days, we'd gone from that easy, immaterial play to having to defend our relationship—*relationship?*—to onlookers.

Noah tugged my hand, and I looked up at him before glancing over to where our visitor had stood. She'd left while I'd been in my own world. I opened my mouth to say something—what, I didn't know. Between my totally uncharacteristic feelings of jealousy and the uncertainty of whatever the fuck there was between Noah and me, I didn't know anything.

"Good evening, Pastor Noah," the waiter said, interrupting whatever nonsense had been about to come out of my mouth. "Harper. Nice to see you both, and sorry about the wait. Can I interest you in a bottle of wine?"

Wine. Yes. Perhaps a little alcohol would give me some clarity over what the hell I'd gotten myself into.

———

Getting tipsy at dinner was the best idea I'd had in a while, allowing me to leave all my worries and uncertainties back at the restaurant. Well, it was my best idea right after leaving my panties in my office and taunting Noah yesterday in front of his church. And also after taking his suggestion and leaving those off tonight when I answered the door for our date.

Okay, so mostly, my best ideas revolved around things that led to Noah giving me lots and lots of orgasms. And if I had my way, that would only continue now that we'd made it back to my place.

I unlocked the door and walked inside, tugging Noah along behind me. He hadn't let go of my hand since we'd left the restaurant. He was a touchy-feely one, that was for sure. Hand-holding shouldn't have been erotic, but somehow, he made it so. Gentle touches, soft caresses, just enough teasing to get me thinking about what would happen later…

"Thank you for spending the evening with me," Noah said, closing the door behind us. "I hope you had a nice time."

I dropped his hand, then raised an eyebrow, pulling the hem of my fitted shirt out of the waistband of my skirt. "That sounds an awful lot like you're getting ready to leave…" I tugged off my shirt, tossing it somewhere in the vicinity of my couch. "What if I'm not ready for the night to be done just yet?"

He didn't drop his eyes to take in any of the skin I'd just exposed. Not even once. He kept his gaze locked on mine as he prowled toward me. "What did you have in mind? I play a mean Jenga, you know."

I breathed out a laugh. How could he make me laugh when I was dying to get him inside me? "Do you play a lot of strip Jenga?" With a quick flick of my fingers, I unhooked my bra, then sent it flying in the direction of my shirt.

"Not usually, no." He put his hand on top of mine, stilling me as I attempted to unzip my skirt. Brushing my hand out of the way, he slid the zipper down, his lips a soft caress against my bare shoulder. "Teach me the rules?"

I tilted my head to the side, encouraging his exploration. I wanted those lips all over me. "In strip Jenga, it's more about sliding things in than pulling out."

He pushed my skirt down until it pooled at my feet, then he clutched my hips, slipping his fingers under the straps of my garters as he pulled me closer. "Slide in. Got it. So how do we determine a winner?"

Teeth, tongue, lips…he was everywhere, all over my neck, sucking on my collarbone, licking a path up to my jaw, nipping at my ear. I couldn't move, couldn't breathe, couldn't *think*.

"Harper."

"Hmm?"

Though I couldn't see him, I could feel his lips curve against my neck. "The winner… How do we know who wins?"

Right. Strip Jenga. "Whoever comes first loses."

He pulled back and looked down at me, tracing a finger around my lips. "That'll be you, doll. Definitely, and more than once."

"Is that a challenge?"

"No." He cupped my breasts in his hands, slowly leading me backward until we were behind the partition separating the living space from my bedroom. Then he gently tugged on my nipple piercings, his smile growing when I gasped. "It's a promise."

Considering our previous encounters, I believed it, too. Despite having been years since he'd been with a woman, he could play me like he'd been doing so his whole life. But that didn't mean I couldn't tease him along the way.

"What are you hiding under all these button-up shirts, Pastor No?" I whispered against his ear, playing with his collar. "Trying to make the congregation think you aren't a red-blooded male under those pressed shirts and pleated pants. That you don't fantasize just like the rest of them." I slipped a button through its hole. Then another and another and another until his shirt parted down the front and I could push it off his shoulders. And then I got my first real look at Noah Reid.

He was...delicious. So much male perfection covered by those modest clothes. Broad shoulders transitioned into a toned chest and sculpted abs. A light dusting of dark hair covered his pecs, and I wanted to feel it against my hands...my breasts. Then I wanted to get my mouth into the mix and lick every inch of him.

He let me look my fill as he stood still as stone, his chest rising and falling in a regulated rhythm. So controlled. Like he was trying to hold back.

That just wouldn't do.

Bracing my hands on his chest, swirling my fingers through the light smattering of hair, I pushed up on my tiptoes and nipped at his bottom lip before soothing the sting with my tongue. "Tell me, Noah. What do you fantasize about?"

He gripped my hips, pulling me closer. Digging his fingers in deep. "You. It doesn't matter what. It's always you."

"For how long?" I didn't know what purpose his answer would serve, but I was suddenly desperate to know. Had he had this infatuation with me the same as I'd had with him? Could he still remember how we'd first met? When I hadn't realized he was the new pastor as he'd offered me his umbrella to protect me from the rain, uncaring about getting drenched himself. I'd wanted nothing more than to pull him into my car and fuck him right then and there. I could pretend my attraction hadn't been immediate and visceral, but I'd only be lying to myself. It'd been an undeniable build between us, the chemistry too potent to be contained. Until yesterday when it'd just…combusted.

"Since the first day in the parking lot. You were so beautiful…and wet." He brushed a finger down my neck to my breast before tracing soft as silk circles around a nipple. "I love it when you're wet."

He reached around, gripping my ass in both his hands, and hauled me up against him. Taking my mouth in a kiss, he slid his tongue against mine as he lowered us to the bed. He tasted like wine and the tiniest hint of chocolate from our dessert. Pure heaven.

I opened my legs for him to settle between, the rough material of his pants brushing against me. I didn't care that I was nearly naked save for my stockings and garters and he was partially clothed. That I was no doubt leaving a trail of wetness over the front of his pants. All I cared about was getting him inside me again.

Noah cupped my breasts in his palms, his thumbs flicking back and forth over my nipples, tugging on my barbells. I gasped when he brought his mouth into play, sucking one hardened peak between his lips, circling his tongue around and around and around until I thought I'd die of pleasure.

No longer able to just lie back, I slid my hands over every inch of him I could reach—into his mess of hair, over his shoulders, down his arms as his biceps flexed under my palms. Trailed my fingers down his chest, over his nipples to the hills and valleys that made up his abs, until I hooked my fingers into the waistband of his gray slacks. Desperate to get him uncovered, feel him inside me, I tried to pry open the button.

"Wait." He covered my hand with his, inadvertently stilling it against his cock. With a groan, he pressed into my hold a bit, and I gave him a squeeze.

"For what? Feels like you're ready to go."

"You come first, remember?" He lowered his face to mine, kissing me once more. "I want it to be on my mouth."

Oh, hell yes. Where moments before I could only think about getting him inside me, now all I could think about was what it'd feel like to come on his tongue.

He kissed a path down my stomach, stopping to swirl his tongue around my belly button, taking a detour to scrape his teeth over my hip. And then he placed his hands on my inner thighs and spread me wide for him, those broad shoulders settling between my legs, and just…stared.

"I've dreamed of doing this to you for months. Of tasting you." He turned his head to the side, brushing his lips over my thigh before sinking his teeth in hard enough to make me jump. "There's no way in hell I can be gentle."

"Then don't be."

With a groan, he dove in. No preamble. No working me up. No teasing. He covered me with his mouth, his tongue working fast and furious against me. Long licks up the length of my slit, followed by fast, hard flicks back and forth against my clit.

And then added his fingers to the mix.

He had me on the edge so fast, flying straight toward my orgasm, I couldn't tell up from down, couldn't discern his fingers from his tongue from his teeth. All I knew was he was devouring me whole. And I absolutely loved it.

"Oh God, you're gonna make me come. *Noah*…"

He groaned against me, working his tongue faster. With a moan, I arched off the bed and reached for his hair, holding him to me as I pressed myself harder against his face. He responded to my moan with one of his own, the sound vibrating against my pussy, and then I was in free fall. Colors burst behind my closed eyelids as I came and came and came…the orgasm drawn out near to the point of discomfort. But Noah didn't stop. He continued his assault on me, not slowing in the slightest. He cupped my ass in his hands and brought me closer to his face, doubling down on his efforts as he worked me right back up again until another orgasm overtook me.

I gasped, unable to speak, to groan, to do anything but remember how to breathe as this man brought me pleasure I'd never known. I rode out the waves of my second orgasm to lightening swipes of Noah's tongue. Then he brushed his mouth over me, back and forth, the tickle of the stubble he'd let grow in creating delicious friction against my clit. I didn't know if I wanted to press closer or pull away, but Noah made the decision for me.

"Hope you don't take the loss too hard, but there was no way I was coming without you going first. That's never going to happen." He pulled away, wiping his forearm across his mouth, and stood, stripping off his slacks and boxers in a rush while I stared. It was the first time I'd seen him completely naked, and I relished every second of it, letting my eyes do a slow sweep over him.

I'd felt him inside me, knew intimately exactly how blessed he was in that department, but laying eyes on the thick inches of flesh and steel in front of me was something else entirely. I wanted to get my hands on him. I wanted to get my *mouth* on him. But before I could do either, he covered himself with a condom and settled on his knees on the edge of the bed.

With quick movements, he stripped me of my remaining articles of clothing, the garter belt and stockings I still wore tossed somewhere to the side. Even with the efficiency with which he moved to get me naked, it didn't feel cheap or rushed. He was still tender in his touches, his eyes caressing me every second.

When I was naked, he smoothed his palms from my ankles to my knees, tugging me closer to him as he hooked my legs over his thighs. Vulnerable and completely open to him. At his mercy with nowhere to hide.

"Is it still considered *strip* Jenga if we're both already naked?" he asked.

The surprised laugh he pulled from me quickly turned to a moan as he pressed inside. Forget Sunday church services or Bible study or prayer groups—when Noah slid into me, his eyes locked on mine, it was the only kind of religious experience I needed. He rocked into me slow and steady, making the rest of the world fall away. Filling me over and over, he caressed every inch of me he could reach, bending down to suck a nipple, taking my mouth in a heated kiss.

"Need you closer." He slid his hands under my back and lifted until I was settled in his lap, my legs wrapped around his hips. "Want to watch you do the heavy lifting for a bit."

I wasn't normally a fan of this position. It was too close…too intimate. It allowed your partner access to every inch of you. Something Noah took advantage of. He ran his hands over my legs, gently encircling my ankles with his fingers. He gripped my ass, tugging me closer, cupped my breasts and drove me crazy with his mouth.

After running his hands up the length of my spine, he threaded his fingers through my hair and tugged my head back to feast on my neck. Intermixing soft kisses with teeth and tongue, he continued to rock inside me, bringing us both to a slow climax.

And when it hit, when he braced his hand at the base of my spine, holding me to him and grinding so deep I had no choice but to fall, I knew it was different. Every second with him was different, from the teasing to the sex. From the way he looked at me to how he kissed me. If I'd been paying attention, I would've seen it'd been different all along.

"Harper…" Even the way he whispered my name was something I'd never known.

When he came apart in my arms, my name a prayer on his lips, I knew whatever I'd thought this had been between us was a lie. Noah was all in.

Strangely, so was I.

chapter seven

WARM. Harper's skin was so warm against mine, so soft and plush. Sharing a bed with her was an extravagance I'd never expected to get to enjoy. It was the pinnacle of my desires, the impossible dream I'd had since the day I met her. And yet, there we were. She had her back to me, her arm pulling mine underneath her pillow to support her head. My leg was between hers, my hand resting on her stomach. In that moment, she was mine… Completely.

Unable to stop myself, to resist touching more, I traced patterns on her skin. I kept my touch innocent at first. Then I moved a little higher on my passes, allowing myself to caress the flesh of her breasts. To slide up to her nipples. Pierced. Of course she was pierced. I'd nearly come in my pants when I finally saw the silver jewelry glinting in the light after feeling them through her clothes. I hadn't gotten nearly as much time to play with them as I wanted. An error I intended to correct.

With my face buried in her neck, her lilac scent driving me absolutely wild with desire, I explored her pierced nipples—tugging, rolling, pinching. Seeking a response. I wanted Harper awake. Well, not just awake. I wanted her wet and slippery as I plunged my cock inside her. Wanted my name on her lips as she came around me. Wanted the taste of her on my tongue as she soaked my chin again.

The first sign that I was well on my way to waking my sleeping doll was a small groan and a shift of her hips closer to me. Her ass—so round, so fucking biteable—pressed into the cradle of my hips, giving my needy cock a good, long rub. I practically growled in her ear, leaning over her, tweaking that fucking nipple again. Wishing I could taste it. Wanting my mouth on her.

"Noah," she groaned, rocking back against me harder as her arm came up to hold the back of my head. She pulled me closer, and I responded. Rolling her over onto her stomach. Biting down on her neck as I covered her body with mine.

"Condom," I said, pressing her into the mattress. Fuck, I wanted to be inside her. Wanted to feel every inch of her. I needed it.

"Nightstand."

I stretched and yanked open the drawer, finding her stash. In seconds, I was sheathed and ready, my heartbeat pulsing through my cock as I slowed down.

Anticipation was a thing, and I wanted her to feel it. Wanted her to grow antsy and desperate. I wanted her to crave me.

It took Harper mere seconds to lose her patience. "Fuck me already, Noah."

I always had done what I was told. Without another delay, I bit down on her neck and pushed inside. Heat. So much heat. And the pressure of her pussy enveloping me. She was so tight, especially with her legs as close together as they were. I'd never had a woman like this, never laid my body on top of hers, pushed myself inside her, and simply took. Never had I allowed myself to overpower a woman, trusting they'd tell me if I went too far. Harper opened doors and opportunities I hadn't expected, and I loved every second. Loved being bold and daring with her, loved the openness and sexual freedom she represented. To be honest, I loved her. I just couldn't tell her that yet. But I could show her. I could demonstrate my care and concern with my body until she was ready for the rest of me. If she was ever ready for the rest of me.

I'd make sure she was ready.

"Everything about you is so soft," I said, breathing harder as I fought to keep control. Unable to resist, I slid a hand beneath her body, moving to cup her breast. To flick the barbell through her nipple. "Except these. There's nothing soft about your piercings."

"Noah…" She moaned, pushing her hips up. Forcing me to slide deeper inside of her. "Pinch them."

I twisted her nipple between my fingers and pressed deeper inside of her. Making her jump and gasp at the dual stimulation. "Next time, I want you on top. I can't wait to get my tongue on these while you fuck yourself on my cock."

"Jesus, I love your mouth."

She felt too good to concentrate on anything other than my cock in her pussy. The warmth, the wetness, the tension surrounding me—it all came together to create a world where there was nothing else. Only her and me and the noises we made as I fucked her long and deep. She mewled and clutched at the sheets, her scent still teasing me. I would never look at those purple flowers again, never be able to walk by a bush of them without getting hard. They were inevitably entwined in my mind with Harper and sex.

Harper gasped as I bit down on her neck again, her arms stretching out before her as if to hold us in place. "I'm… Fuck, I'm gonna come."

Hand on the headboard to anchor us to the mattress, I thrust hard and deep, rocking the bed into the wall as I did. The squeaks and bangs added to the feeling of a fury approaching, cut out the rest of the world completely as I led us both toward where we wanted to be. Where we needed to be. This was it…us. Together. Our pleasure intertwined, our lives wrapping around one another.

This was everything.

Harper came with a moan, her pussy clenching around me as her body went stiff. She squeezed me so hard and yelled so loud, I thought I heard bells with every heartbeat and pulse. Eyes closed, ears ringing, I slammed into her until the telltale tingle at the base of my spine moved down and through my cock. One more thrust, one more push. Just a little…

I crashed right after her, pushing deeper and stilling as I did, growling through the longest, hardest orgasm of my life. Stars exploded behind my eyes, colors lighting up the blackness, and those bells grew louder. I was completely surrounded by her, owned by the heat of her. Dominated by the scent and feel of her. There would never be more than this, never be anyone who compared to her. Never be another who could make me feel the same way, physically or emotionally. I was hers. I just needed to make sure she knew that.

"Wow," Harper said, laughing slightly as she wiggled beneath me. I groaned and pulled out of her, rolling to the side to deal with the condom. Once done, I pulled her back to my chest and wrapped my arms all the way around her. I still wanted her touch, still craved the feel of her skin against mine.

"Yeah. Wow." I snuggled her close, needing a moment more of contact. Focusing on her breaths and the feel of her fingers skating over my arms. If only I could get my ears to stop ringing…

"Is that the church?" Harper asked, rocking back into me as if trying to turn over.

"I've never had a woman call my dick 'the church,' but I'll take it."

"No." She laughed, reaching back to playfully slap my thigh. "The bells."

It took a few seconds for her words to filter

through the fog around my brain, but when they did…

"Shit." I jumped up, running for the front window of the apartment. Cars…lots of them. Including ones belonging to the people who were technically my bosses. "Double shit."

"What's wrong?"

"It's Tuesday. I'm supposed to be at the church to welcome everyone for the hour of silent reflection. The entire council is coming." I yanked on my clothes, or those I could find. I'd have to leave my socks behind, apparently. Those bells meant I had five minutes before the hour would begin. Not enough time to make a cup of coffee, but enough to run to my office and brush my teeth in the washroom. Hopefully.

"You're leaving? Just like that?"

Shit, I was being an ass. I dove back onto the bed for one last quick kiss. "I know this seems bad, but I need to go to work. Thanks for last night. It was amazing."

I rushed for the door, practically running out of the apartment. Refusing to look back. If I saw her all warm and sex-rumpled in those sheets, knowing she was naked and probably still sloppy wet, I'd be right back on top of her. If she asked me to, I'd never leave her side. I just had the one service to perform, the one council meeting to deal with afterward, and then I could come back. Maybe I'd take her out for brunch or coffee. Maybe…

"I'll see you later, doll," I said just before the door to her apartment closed behind me. Later…just a few hours…then I could be with her again. I raced down the stairs and jogged across the street, heading for the back door of the church. I ran into trouble in the parking lot, though, in the form of one of the church council members and his wife.

"Pastor Noah," Henry said, looking me up and down as if surprised to see me coming from across the street. Not that I could blame him. I wasn't dressed for any sort of church function, and I probably looked as if I'd just rolled out of bed. Which I had. After fucking the woman of my dreams.

"Henry. Marge. It's a good morning for reflection, don't you think?"

"Are you"—Henry's wife Marge glanced behind me at Harper's store, her face white and her eyes round—"are you coming from Sin?"

Sin…yeah. That was what we'd been doing. Harper and I had been sinning. I couldn't wait to do more of it, either.

"No, of course not." I grinned, unable to hold it back. "I'm coming from Miss Davis' place."

That certainly didn't make her look any less surprised. "Harper Davis? The owner of…that store?"

"Yes. We're dating." The silence that greeted me from the two of them couldn't even touch the joy I felt after last night. Let them talk—Harper was mine, and they'd stop gossiping once they realized I was serious about her. I had faith in that. "Well, if you'll excuse me, I need to grab a few things from my office before the service begins. See you in there."

I left them staring after me as I headed for the

church. I had about two minutes to get myself ready for the day. Thankfully, Tuesdays weren't all that busy for me. Just a few hours, and I could be back with Harper, which was where I wanted to be. But my duties were clear, and these hours of reflection were something the community really seemed to enjoy. Besides, sitting in silence the way I would be for the next hour meant I could reflect on my night with Harper. I could relive every moan and sigh, every touch and taste. I could plan for what I wanted to do to her tonight.

One hour of reflection, then probably two of council meetings. That was it.

I'd be counting down the minutes until I could be back with my girl for sure.

chapter eight

HARPER

I STARED AT the closed door for a full minute after Noah blew out of it without even a backward glance. After he'd just fucked me into the mattress. After a night unlike any I'd known. After I'd let him get closer than anyone ever had before.

I was naked, lying in a bed of rumpled sheets… alone. Stunned. I didn't get caught off guard very often, but Noah had managed to do just that, throwing me way off-balance.

But this was exactly what I'd always wanted. What had always worked for me… Being left, alone, after a night of amazing sex. I'd spent my life seeking exactly that, had always been satisfied with it. No strings, no commitments, no relationships.

So why was my stomach churning? Why was there this hollow feeling inside? Even though my body still ached with awareness of exactly where Noah had been and what he'd done last night—and again this morning—I'd never before felt this empty.

I hadn't spent the night with a man in…well, ever, so I was probably just a little off my game. Especially considering I'd closed my eyes for only a moment last night and then suddenly woken up this morning in Noah's arms, his hands cupping my breasts, his cock hard and ready against me. It'd been languorous… affectionate. Two things I never thought I'd equate with sex. It was definitely a first for me—just like the sleepy morning sex.

But it was no big deal. Just sex. Noah's passing remark before he fled proved how he saw it—as a single day between us. The same way I did. An amazing day and one I wouldn't soon forget, but still just one day.

I turned my head, burying my face in my pillow, only to realize it smelled like Noah. My blanket did, too. Even my *hair* smelled like him. With a groan, I threw off the covers and pushed myself out of bed because it was driving me crazy that his scent surrounded me. Like he'd never left.

After a quick shower, I slipped into my favorite dress and pulled my hair back into a cute ponytail, then painted my lips with my favorite color. It was a red lipstick kind of day.

I had a bit of time before I needed to be downstairs to open the store, so I stripped my bedding and threw it in the washing machine before remaking the bed with fresh linens.

And then it was like Noah had never even been there.

It was surprising how easily any trace of him could be removed from my life. Had it really only been forty-eight hours since this whole thing between us had come to a head? Because it felt like a lifetime.

I poured myself some coffee into my travel mug and grabbed my e-reader, making sure it was stocked with reading material in case it was slow today. With one last glance at my apartment, completely wiped clean of any evidence of last night, I shut the door behind me and headed down the steps on the side of the building.

The sun was bright, the air crisp but not chilly. Another beautiful fall day on the island, and people were out enjoying it. Cars filled the church parking lot—a typical scene for Tuesdays, as one of the busier days at the church. I normally reveled in their busy days, when visitors would pour out of the front doors, the red awning above Sin immediately drawing their gazes. I'd stand outside under the guise of watering my flowers and flutter my fingers in the direction of those grouchy old women. Women who walked around with perpetual wedgies because they constantly got their panties in a twist anytime they even saw me walk down the street.

Today, however, I couldn't bring myself to give the church more than a cursory glance on my way to the front of my building. The thought of seeing Noah after he ran out just an hour before made my stomach twist with something I definitely hadn't had enough coffee to examine.

Actually, come to think of it, that examination might be better suited for the gin variety.

I juggled my e-reader and coffee, readying my keys as I approached the front door of Sin.

"Harper!"

On instinct, I turned my head in the direction of my name. Noah stood across the street, members of his congregation surrounding him. When our eyes connected, he smiled and waved, then left the people talking to him and jogged toward me. He still wore the clothes he'd had on last night, every bit as rumpled as I'd expect them to be from spending an evening shoved between my couch cushions or under my bed.

The thought caused my stomach to flip, remembering his face buried between my legs. How he'd taken me, soft and sweet, yet still somehow greedy. How he'd pulled me into his lap, taking the opportunity to run his fingers or his palms or his lips over every inch of me he could.

Then I remembered how he'd fucked me this morning, then bailed with little more than a thank you.

Straightening my spine, I glanced behind Noah toward the people still crowding the front lawn of the church, all eyes on us. "Pastor Noah."

His smile faltered as his brow drew down. "I was hoping I'd run into you. I'm sorry I had to rush off this morning."

I nearly laughed because it was usually me who was feeding some bullshit line. I waved him off, needing to get into the sanctuary of my store. Needing some space from Noah. "I get it. Lots to do on weekdays for the pastor." I turned away, finding the key I needed for the shop. "I'll see you around, Noah."

"Hey, stop for a second." He reached out to still me, encircling my wrist and pulling me out of the alcove of the entryway. I glanced down at his hand, hating how much I loved feeling his fingertips against my pulse point. Hating how it reminded me of his intimate touches at dinner last night. "I really am sorry. I forgot all about reflection this morning."

"Well, I'll give you one thing—I've certainly never gotten that excuse before."

"It's not an excuse. I wanted to stay in bed with you, but the silent reflection hour is one of our biggest weekday events. I couldn't miss it without someone to stand in for me." He tightened his grip, his thumb rubbing circles against the underside of my wrist. "Please. Let me take you to lunch. We can—damn, I have a church council thing. Dinner, then. Let me take you out to dinner again."

I shook my head, pulling my hand away, because I couldn't think when he was touching me. "I don't think that's a good idea."

His brow furrowed, confusion plain on his face. "I'm not sure I understand."

"Look, Noah, I get it. We're both adults. You had a little itch to scratch, and who better to scratch it with than me, right?"

"You are not just an itch, Harper."

"An itch. A little acting out. Whatever you want to call it."

Voices carried from across the street, drawing my attention, only to find nearly everyone outside looking in our direction. Some of them were covert about it, slight nods toward us, while others were just outright pointing at the two of us together.

I put on my best smile and waved to the catty, gossipy bastards. To Noah, I said, "We've got an audience."

He shook his head, not sparing them a glance. "I don't care about them. I'm here to talk to you."

"I'm not exactly thrilled to have my personal business discussed in front of the people who have no problem judging me day in and day out, so I'd really rather not."

"Harper, I don't—"

"If you'll excuse me, I need to open the shop. Goodbye, Noah."

"Harper, wait. Let's go inside and talk. There has to be a way—"

"Everything okay, Pastor Noah?"

"Henry, this isn't a good time."

"Yes, I can see that. But the council is convening—"

I didn't stick around to hear the rest, slipping into the shop and locking the front door behind me. I had thirty minutes until I needed to flip the front sign to OPEN, and I was going to use every single one of them.

Their muted voices seeped through the walls, low enough that I couldn't discern what they were saying. I walked around the counter and placed my stuff down before going to the register to ready it for the day. From here, I had a perfect view out the front window to where Noah stood with Henry, husband of one of the gossipier blue-hairs I had to deal with. Noah said something to him, then glanced back to where I'd been standing moments ago. He closed his eyes, his shoulders sagging as he looked at the empty patch of concrete.

The soft hum of a voice filtered into the store again. Noah turned back to Henry, and he nodded.

And then he walked away.

chapter nine

MY PATIENCE WAS waning.

For hours, I'd done everything I was supposed to do—I'd led the hour of reflection, I'd counseled one of the local youth who had stopped by unannounced looking for guidance, I'd answered phone calls and offered prayers. Dealing with the church council—the governing body of the congregation—was getting on my last nerve.

"Pastor Noah, I'm not sure you're understanding our concerns."

I glared up at the man in question, the one who had never been supportive of anything I'd wanted to do for the congregation. "Considering you've reiterated them six times now, I'm pretty sure I've got them."

Charlie, the president of the council and usually one of the more progressive members, sighed. "Henry,

I'm going to have to agree with Noah here. You've voiced your concerns over the pastor's social life. Why don't we move on to other business?"

But there was no other business, and everyone staring at me from the other side of the table knew it. We were here solely because Henry and his wife were now aware Harper and I were an item and didn't like it. I knew how people talked about her, knew there would be chatter among some of the more closed-minded townspeople. I hadn't expected it to be so soon, though. And I hadn't expected to be unsure of my relationship's viability with her when the shit hit the fan.

"Pastor Noah?" Charlie said, regaining my attention.

"What?"

"I just wondered if there was anything else you'd like to say before we close out this emergency session?"

Yes. I wanted to read to them from the Bible, to quote the scriptures regarding how Jesus chose to treat others around him. Wanted to sermonize on kindness and withholding judgment, on the good found in someone's heart and the evils of forcing your views on others. There was a lot I wanted to say, but first, I needed to get to Harper. I needed to fix whatever the hell had happened in front of her shop this morning.

"No," I said, taking to my feet. "I have things to do."

"You mean like shaving?" Henry asked, the implication clear in his voice.

I turned slowly on my heel, unable not to. "Is that really what you want to discuss here? My grooming habits? I realize your wife has had some sort of obsession with the infrequency of my shaving, Henry, but I didn't realize that had bled over into you as well. So let's deal with this."

I stepped closer to the table, opening my arms in invitation and letting my pastor voice gain volume. "I don't shave during the week. That's a capitulation to this very council, who didn't want a pastor with facial hair. If it were up to me, I'd have a beard right now. But I compromised. You all might want to look up the definition of that word and find your own places to compromise."

All five of them seemed to find the paper in front of them very important in that moment, the cowards. But if they thought I was done, they were wrong. Very, very wrong.

"I'd like to remind you all that my sermons are strong and well received, the pews are filled for every service on Sunday, and the offerings are far exceeding expectations. I won't be nitpicked, and I certainly won't allow anyone on this island or beyond to insinuate there is something inherently sinful about Harper Davis. I fully intend to continue speaking the word of the Lord in the manner I see reaching the people of this community, and I definitely intend to live up to the credo of love thy neighbor when it comes to Miss Davis."

I grabbed my notebook, too angry give a thought to procedures and policies. They'd crossed a line, and I refused to slink away without them understanding that. "If you want to be petty enough to imply I'm not the right leader for this congregation simply because of my lack of shaving or whom I choose to date, then perhaps you should consider convening a committee to find another pastor. Now, if you'll excuse me."

I let the door slam behind me as I stalked out into the hallway. Enough was enough. I could handle the jokes about looking young and the side comments about my weekday beard. I dealt with long hours and little pay, with apathy and lack of empathy for people within their own community. I would not—could not—deal with anyone attacking Harper simply because I chose to date her. She was joy personified, light and hope in one hell of a package.

And she was angry with me.

When I finally made it outside, I nearly howled in frustration. Sin was busy. Too busy for me to go barging in and demand Harper stop doing her job just to appease me. That would go over like a lead balloon. I'd need to wait for a bit, give the place time to clear out. Maybe give myself time to collect my thoughts.

"Pastor Noah?"

Or give people time to track me down. "Officer Nash. It's good to see you."

"You all right? You look a little…"

Yeah, I was sure I did. "I'm fine. I was hoping to go see Miss Davis about something, but I don't want to interrupt her customers."

"It's Jane's Hour tonight."

"Pardon?"

"Jane's Hour…like Jane Doe? Harper brings in

different speakers to host discussions for victims of sexual assault. Tonight, it's a sex therapist who wrote some book about reclaiming your sexuality after abuse. I volunteered for guard duty since it's so dark when the meetings end. We like to make sure the ladies all make it to their cars safely."

"Right. I forgot." Well, now I definitely couldn't interrupt her until I knew her evening was over. Not when she was doing something so important and needed in the community. The lingering doubt was going to kill me, though.

"You okay, Pastor?" Connor asked, cocking his head as he looked me over.

I couldn't imagine what he saw as an officer of the law—I was still wearing my clothes from the day before, still hadn't had time to brush my hair or wash my face, and I was probably twitching like a junkie looking for his next fix after having been away from Harper for so long.

Shit, he'd asked me a question.

"I'm sorry," I said, shaking my head. "It's been a long day. I'm…" But I didn't have an answer for him. How could I? Societal norms dictated that I should tell him I was fine and be done with it, but was I? No, I wasn't fine. Far from it. Angry? Yes, slightly. Frustrated? Totally. Hurt?

Exponentially.

Connor gave me one more look then seemed to relax. "If you weren't a pastor, I'd say you need a beer."

I shot a glance across the street to the shop where

my Harper was inside, doing good work. "You know what? I do need a beer."

He laughed and clapped a hand on my shoulder. "Then maybe you should get one. Since you're home and all."

"Want to join me?"

"Next time. I've got to keep an eye out tonight." He turned as if to leave, but before he took more than two steps, he swung back around. "Pastor?"

"Yeah?"

"She's a good person." He nodded toward Sin. "Don't ever let the pearl-clutchers brigade make you think otherwise. Harper does a lot for Temperance Falls—for the women, specifically. She's a gift to the community, and no one had better say different around me."

Sometimes words were just words, but other times, they were a map leading you to the place you needed to be. While I'd been upset about how things had played out with Harper today, I'd forgotten to consider my actions through her eyes. The woman who had to fight every day to be accepted, the one who was stared at, who built another layer of protection around herself when people started to whisper about her. I'd left her naked in her bed with little more than an offhanded comment and a kiss on the cheek.

I was an idiot.

"Thank you for the reminder. I needed that tonight."

"Any time." Connor nodded once, then headed toward Sin once more. "Enjoy your beer."

But beer was no longer on my mind. Instead, I was focused on the amazing woman across the street who deserved so much more respect than she was getting. And how I was going to do whatever it took to make her mine.

chapter ten

IT WAS DUMB and naïve, but I'd actually thought Noah would come back last night. I'd pretended I hadn't been looking out the front window of the shop all evening in hopes of seeing him, had even lied to Gen about it. But I couldn't lie to myself.

How the hell had I let this happen?

True, Noah and I had been circling each other since that first day more than a year ago, our entire relationship the longest streak of foreplay in history, starting the moment I laid eyes on him. Last night while I'd lain in a bed completely stripped of his presence, I still hadn't been able to get away from him. I'd stared at the ceiling, replaying every minute of the previous night, and come to a startling conclusion: During each and every one of our tirades, every verbal match, every bout of flirtatious teasing, we'd been headed somewhere. More importantly, *I'd* been headed somewhere—on a one-way trip to right where I found myself now. A place I'd never intended to go.

In love. With a pastor.

My grandmother had definitely gotten the last laugh. She was no doubt cackling from beyond the grave, pleased that I'd truly fucked myself over this time. Because in the end, love didn't matter. It was never enough to keep people around—I'd learned that before I'd learned my ABC's. Despite declaring her love for me, my grandmother had used me solely as proof of my mother's horrible life choices. And my mom's love had been conditional on the fact that my very existence served to piss off my grandmother.

No one had ever taken me as I was—imperfect and unapologetic about it—and loved me anyway.

I didn't know why I thought Noah would be the exception to the rule.

"Harper!" Gen snapped her fingers in front of my face, pulling me from my thoughts.

"What?"

"Girl, what's going on? I've been trying to get your attention for five minutes." Gen tossed her purse behind the counter and tugged off her coat. "Does it have something to do with the delicious pastor? Because I heard—"

"No talk of Pastor No, please."

Like the good employee she was, she threw back her head and laughed. "That's cute how you think I'm gonna drop it." She perched on a stool, her elbow on the counter, chin in hand, and leaned toward me. "Not happening. Not after what I just heard."

I rolled my eyes, because I could only imagine what sort of gossip had infested the island. By now, the rumors probably had Noah and me fucking in the pews after Sunday service. "I definitely don't want to know."

"Um, yeah ya do." She nodded, her head bouncing like a bobblehead. "You definitely, *definitely* do."

"Look, Gen, it's been a shitty twenty-four hours. I'm not interested in whatever bullshit the blue-hairs have come up with to desecrate my reputation, and I def—"

"Okay, but how about the part where Pastor No basically told the council to fuck off when they told him to stop dating you? Can we talk about that?"

Mouth agape, I blinked at her. Blinked again. "He *what?*"

"Yep. When I was at Bundt and Grind this morning, I heard Marge telling Norma about it. Apparently, Marge's husband is on the council?" Gen waved a dismissive hand. "Anyway, I guess Noah tried to walk away from the discussion, calling the whole thing ridiculous, but they pushed, and then he just kind of snapped. He went on a tirade about how their actions weren't becoming of the Christians they proclaimed to represent and then defended you and the store and your presence on the island. And then he stormed out, like some kind of pastoral badass. *God,* can you imagine how hot he must've looked while doing that?"

Yeah, I could imagine. Noah was laid-back most of the time, but I'd had a front row seat to exactly what happened when you pushed him too far. And apparently, they'd pushed him too far.

"You guys seriously didn't talk about it?" Gen asked.

"No...I haven't seen him since yesterday morning."

"Then what are you doing in here? He's looking mighty fine out front, all sweaty and manly, doing your heavy lifting for you."

I whipped my head to stare out the front window, and sure enough, there he was. Wearing a white T-shirt plastered to his chest and broken-in jeans encasing powerful thighs, he moved one of the huge planters I'd used only as a ruse to irritate him the other day. Standing there, he looked so reminiscent of that first time I'd seen him in the parking lot last fall, except instead of rain forming his shirt to his chest, today it was sweat. From doing my work for me.

After placing a planter directly under the front window, he turned around and started for the other. Jesus, that shirt might as well be nonexistent for all it did to conceal the muscles flexing in his back as he wiped a forearm across his brow before bending to lift the other planter.

"Not sure what you're still doing standing in here, but I've got the store." Gen lifted her chin in the direction of the front door, a huge grin splitting her face. "Go have a chat with your man."

My man. Not quite, but I couldn't think about that. In fact, I didn't stop to think about anything.

Not what I'd say or what I'd do. Didn't consider the consequences of what might come from me pushing through the door and standing there, outside, in front of prying eyes as Noah placed the second planter to the right of the front door.

It wouldn't have mattered, though. Because when he stood to his full height, exhaling a deep breath, every thought fell out of my head, and all I could see was him.

"Good morning," he said, glancing to the planters before meeting my eyes again. "I wasn't sure where you wanted them, but I remember they were hugging the door in some pictures of the town from last Christmas."

I honestly didn't care where the planters were. Had never cared. "Thank you. You didn't have to do that."

"I know I didn't have to, but I wanted to." He didn't try to hide how he looked me over, his gaze taking in every inch of me. "I needed to make sure you were happy."

When was the last time someone wanted to make sure I was happy? Never. I took a step toward him, bringing us within touching distance. Before I could take another one, movement across the street caught my eye. Marge, wife of council member Henry and all-around gossip, looked on, not bothering to conceal the interest in her gaze.

Lowering my voice to make sure it didn't carry, I asked, "Is that the only reason you came by?"

"No. But I figured it was the most logical excuse to see you, considering."

Caught off guard by his bluntness, I laughed. "Smooth, Pastor No." Without conscious thought, I took another step toward him, near enough that I could feel his breath ghosting over my lips. Being this close to him should have short-circuited my brain, but I couldn't stop darting glances toward Marge, who still stood outside the church, worried about her seeing Noah and me together, considering what had supposedly happened yesterday.

Following my gaze, Noah looked back over his shoulder, his jaw tightening as he saw who was standing there.

Pulling his attention back to me, I reached for his hand. "I heard what you did yesterday. With the council."

"I stand by what I said. If they feel I'm the wrong person for the job, then they should find another pastor to lead them. I'm not afraid to walk away." His voice was hard, insistent, and he tossed a look over his shoulder toward Marge.

"Noah…" I squeezed his hand, trying not to think about how perfectly mine fit inside his. "You could lose your job for this. Is it really worth it?" I didn't say it, couldn't bring myself to, but what I was really asking was, *am* I *worth it?*

His brow furrowed as he brought a hand up to my face, a single finger tracing down my cheek. "When I first came to Temperance Falls, a few of the council members brought up their disappointment in what this shop had become. The choir director at the time pulled me aside and told me the good you do here, though. The therapists for sexual assault survivors, the donations to local organizations helping families in need, the fact that you're discreet and knowledgeable and have probably saved more marriages on the island than any marriage counselor could have. You are a value to this community, Harper, as is this shop. I won't let anyone disparage you or it."

I tried not to let my disappointment show. They were lovely words, but they were words about my store, about my accomplishments—things I never questioned. Nothing about *me*. Nothing about his feelings for whatever this was between us.

"Plus," he said, wrapping an arm around me and tugging me right up against the front of him. "You're the source of my joy. I've been obsessed with you since the first time I saw you carrying those bags in the rain. I was drawn to you from the start, and getting to know you has only intensified my attraction. I know you're not ready, and I know this probably seems too fast, but you are my hope, Harper Davis. I love you, and I know someday I'm going to prove to you that it's okay to love me back."

I could only blink at him, having had every ounce of my voice stolen away. I was twenty-eight, had been with my fair share of men, had had fun while doing so. But I'd never once heard those words from a man. I'd assumed if I ever did, I'd go running in the opposite direction as fast as I could. And yet there I was, aching not to run, but instead to crawl inside him and never leave.

Reaching up, I brushed my hand over the growth

on his jaw, remembering what it felt like against my neck, over the tips of my breasts, between my legs. "You're okay being known as the pastor dating the girl who owns a sex shop? Because I'm not selling it. Ever."

"Absolutely, especially if we get to play with some of the toys now and again."

I laughed, having no idea how I'd managed to find the perfect man, but nonetheless thrilled about it. "I think that can be arranged."

He smiled, then his face grew serious again. "Are you okay with me possibly not being the pastor? Because that could change. I'm not giving you up, so I may be saying goodbye to the church."

There was so much to take in—the fact that this man not only loved me, but was willing to give up everything he knew just to be able to be with me. Going up on my tiptoes, I brushed my lips over his. "I'm not here because you're a pastor. I'm here because you're *Noah*."

What I'd intended to be a brief kiss, something soft and sweet, Noah redirected with ease. He held me to him with a hand gripping my ass and the other cupping the back of my neck. And then he slid his tongue across my lips until I opened for him. With a moan, he took my mouth just like he'd taken me yesterday: thoroughly and possessively.

Pulling back, he ran his thumb over my bottom lip, his eyes once again serious. "I'm just glad you're here at all after yesterday. I never meant to make you feel like I wasn't in this. I completely lose track of time and responsibilities when we're together. Especially when I'm in your…" He trailed off, his hand slipping into the waistband of my skirt, not stopping until his fingers teased my pussy from behind.

I breathed out a laugh. "You certainly know how to make a girl swoon, Pastor No." Smiling, I gripped the neckline of his shirt, tugging him closer to me as I bit my lip to stifle the moan threatening to break free. "Wanna lose some more time now?"

"Definitely. But not out here." He slipped his hand free, causing me to whimper in frustration. With a knowing smile, he guided me along the front of the building toward the staircase leading to my apartment, waving at Gen as we passed the window as if he hadn't just had his hand on my pussy. Then he leaned in, his lips right next to my ear. "No one else gets to see you the way I do."

I should've hated how he spoke with such possession, but instead, I found myself melting further into him. Because the truth was, I didn't want to share it with anyone else. Just Noah.

"So, what do you say?" he asked. "Another game of strip Jenga?"

I'd always thought being stuck in a relationship would be the death of me. It was something I'd spent my whole life running from. Now that I faced it, though, it was nothing like I'd anticipated. I didn't feel scared or claustrophobic, but instead, I felt invigorated at the thought of spending all my nights with him.

"Absolutely. Let's see if I can win this time…"

epilogue

CHRISTMAS WOULD NEVER be my favorite time of year. While I enjoyed the season and the good it brought out in people, the sheer number of events, plans, and functions I was responsible for as a religious leader was daunting. There were days when I seriously weighed the choice of whether to go home to sleep or simply to camp out in my office. If it wasn't for Harper enticing me at every turn, I doubt I'd have left the church at all that final week leading up to the holiday.

Two more days. I recited the words in my head over and over as I listened to the final practice of the choir. Just Christmas Eve and Christmas Day services left, and then I was off work for two weeks as I recovered from a grueling holiday season. Harper was even taking a break—the two of us heading to a warmer climate where she could wear very little clothing, I could let my beard grow in as much as I wanted, and we could be like any other couple on the beach.

Two more days.

As the choir moved into a haunting version of "Mary, Did You Know," I caught a glimpse of a familiar figure in the very last pew. Lola Perez sat in the shadows, her head bowed in what I assumed was prayer. I moved toward her out of instinct, curious as to why she'd shown up tonight of all nights. Before I could reach her, though, Officer Connor Nash slipped into the church behind Lola. He watched her for a few seconds, his body still and his face concerned, and then he moved to sit beside her. Something in the way she reacted, in how her body moved toward his, indicated a familiarity or friendship there I hadn't been aware of. One I didn't feel comfortable interrupting.

A moment later, Lola and Connor became the furthest things from my mind. Harper had arrived, sneaking into the church from the side door closest to my office. I reacted immediately, zeroing in on her. Rushing to greet her. She was a sight for sore eyes, and I couldn't wait to breathe in her lilac scent. The one that grounded me. That turned me on as well.

Too bad we were in the church.

Harper greeted me with a smile, grabbing my hand and dragging me down the hall toward my office without uttering a word.

"What's this, doll?"

She shrugged, the heavy, dark coat she wore pulling tight across her shoulders. "You have thirty minutes before the council starts arriving for their Christmas dinner and meeting."

"Don't remind me," I said as she pulled me into my office and turned to shut the door behind us. "Are you joining me at the dinner? You know you're invited."

"Hell no, I'm not joining you." She grinned, pushing me to sit on the couch along the wall as her hands moved to the zipper of her coat. Her face was flushed, those blue eyes of hers sparkling in the overhead light. "At least not for dinner."

The expression on her face, the sensual way she moved as she stripped off the heavy overcoat—my doll was ready to play. As tired as I was, as frustrated and stressed, I was all in on her plan. Especially when she dropped the coat to the floor and revealed the most sinful Santa-type costume I'd ever seen.

"Are you my present?" I asked as I reached for her. Harper came willingly, holding a small red velvet bag with fur trim. Her nipples showed through the lace fabric of the bra she wore, the balls of the barbells pierced through her flesh obvious. The matching panties sat low on her hips, the slip of fabric disappearing between her soft thighs. I wanted to follow that fabric with my tongue, to have her sit on my face and let her take her pleasure from me. But this was Harper's show, so I sat back and waited instead. Watching. Staring as she lifted one leg and set her foot beside my hip.

"I like the shoes," I murmured, running my hand up the white stockings with sparkly things along the side. She tilted her leg, giving me a good view of the bright red heel with silent silver bells hanging from the front. Wait…was that mistletoe?

"I thought you might. You know the legend about mistletoe, don't you?"

I flicked the edge of the green leaf tucked under the bell. "You have to kiss underneath it."

"That's your rule. At Sin, we take things a little further." She leaned closer, her hips almost directly in front of my face. Naughty little elf.

"Are you feeling needy, doll?" I ran my hand up her thigh, wrapping my fingers around the edge of her panties and tugging them to the side. "I can help you out with that, you know."

"I do know." She crawled into my lap, one leg on either side of me. Straddling my hips and rubbing her pussy over my cock, which was straining to be let free from my khakis.

Flat front—Harper made me burn the pleated ones.

I grabbed her ass with both hands, rubbing hard. Kneading it as she reached between us to unfasten my pants. In seconds, the tan fabric was halfway down my thighs, and Harper was back to rubbing herself over my cock. Teasing me. Teasing both of us.

"Let me taste you," I murmured as I moved to bite down on her bottom lip. She jerked and sighed, rocking harder, grabbing one of my hands to pull it around her back.

"Not tonight."

I froze, staring up at her. "Are you seriously turning me down?"

She grinned and leaned down to kiss me, tugging my hand behind her again. "You can lick my pussy later. We got in new toys today."

Fuck and yes. Harper, being a good businesswoman, spent a lot of time trying out the various sex toys companies sent her. Vibrators, dildos, plugs, beads…you name it, she'd tried it. Or should I say, we'd tried it. Friday night had officially become our research and development evening, and it was by far my favorite night of the week.

"What did you bring me? A new vibrator? No, that glass dildo you've been eyeing in the catalog on the kitchen counter." I frowned when she shook her head. "What is it, then?"

She tugged my hand again, pulling it between her ass cheeks. I caught the edge of the plug with my fingertip, knocking it, making her shiver. Holy shit, was it…vibrating?

"Do I get to see?" I asked, tapping the hard circle to tease her a little more. Yes, definitely vibrating. Harper nodded and crawled off me, moving to stand against my desk across the room. She tugged her panties down her legs, keeping her eyes on mine before turning around. Back to me, hands planted on the desktop, she spread her legs and shot me the most evil grin over her shoulder. And then she bent at the waist.

"I thought the red stone at the base was a nice touch. Very festive. What do you think?"

I was up and on her before I could breathe. Fuck…there was a glittering gemstone hidden away back there. The princess plug only added to the hotness that was Harper's amazing ass. If it was the one I assumed it was—the one she'd been talking about for the last month—it had a remote control to turn on and off a vibrating core, the pulsing claiming to increase sensation when used during sex. For both of us.

It was time to find out.

"Bend over," I demanded, pushing her shoulders down with one hand as my other grasped the base of my cock. Harper complied, though I knew I'd catch shit later for ordering her around. That was fine. I deserved it, but she couldn't really blame me when she showed up ready to live out her double-penetration fantasy with me. "Are you sure you want to do this here?"

She nodded, grabbing the edge of the desk as she pressed back against me. "I didn't want to wait. I tried…but the videos for this thing were so fucking hot."

Of course they were. Fuck, the idea of Harper sitting at home, watching videos of people playing with their plugs, her fingers probably buried deep inside her…that was all I needed. I thrust inside slowly, giving both of us time to adjust to the new sensations. And they were new. The vibration added a layer of feeling to her pussy that I'd never experienced, and if her moaning was any indication, the little plug was definitely adding to her pleasure as well as mine. Which was just what we'd hoped for with this particular toy. Harper always felt amazing, and our sex life was filled with adventure and satisfaction, but this was…

"Holy fuck, that vibrator feels so good." She grappled against the desktop, rising up on the balls of her feet to meet my thrusts. Pushing back into me and forcing my cock deeper. "Oh God. I'm going to come so fast."

"Thank fuck for that." I hissed, pushing harder. The plug put pressure on my cock, tightening everything around me. And the tickle of sensation from the vibrator had me pumping into her with rough, frenzied thrusts. Nothing had ever felt this good. I hadn't thought sex with Harper could get better. I'd been wrong.

It took a grand total of about three minutes for Harper to clench down on me, her pussy positively dripping with her release. Face down, mouth pressed against the desktop, she trembled hard as she milked my cock for everything it was worth. I followed right after her, grunting through my own orgasm, laying my body down over hers for more contact. More skin. More of her. More of us together.

I would never get enough.

"This is so coming with us to Jamaica," I said as I finally pulled out of her. Harper dropped a small remote control I hadn't even noticed on my desk, the subtle sound of the vibrator disappearing.

Harper groaned and rolled over, her hair a cloud around her head. "After coming like that, I just might take it everywhere."

I laughed and picked her up, carrying her over to the couch and sitting down with her in my lap. She cuddled close, kissing across the front of my shirt before tucking her head into the crook of my neck.

"Happy Christmas Eve Eve," she said, chuckling.

"That was probably the best gift I've ever received." I kissed the top of her head and pulled her tighter. "Two more days."

"Two more days." She sighed, gripping my arms. "Then it's two weeks on a beach—"

"With you in bikinis every day."

"With me in bikinis every day. And then…" She grinned up at me, looking almost shy about her excitement.

At least she wasn't scared anymore. "And then we come back and move in to the apartment over the store."

"Yeah." Her eyes stayed locked on mine, her smile growing. "You'll be mine every night."

I didn't want to tell her I already was because she'd simply point out it wasn't the same. Moving in together had been a big step for her, a big commitment for the two of us. Not big enough for me. There was a ring hidden in my dresser that proclaimed that fact loudly. But Harper wasn't ready for that, so we'd move in together. And we'd go at her pace for a while. But someday, she'd be all mine. Legally.

I just had to have faith.

She's an original sin sort of bad

I never should've looked at my police officer neighbor the way I did. We were too mismatched, too different to even hope we could be together. Especially seeing as how he could arrest me at any moment for what I did for a living. But Connor couldn't help being my knight in shining armor, and one last rescue makes me lose what little control I had. To be with him, I have to give up my job and, very possibly, my home on the island. Even then, I don't know if he can ever forgive me for the sins I can't wash away.

He's one of the good guys

From the moment Lola moved into my apartment building, I've wanted her. She's too sweet and seemingly innocent, but it doesn't stop me from lusting after her. There's something about the hours she keeps, though. Something about the life she leads that has warning bells going off in my cop brain. Yet I can't stay away. Not when she needs my help. Not when she needs me. Even if being with her could cost me my future.

about the author

London Hale is the combined pen name of writing besties Ellis Leigh and Brighton Walsh. Between them, they've published more than thirty books in the contemporary romance, paranormal romance, and romantic suspense genres. Ellis is a *USA Today* bestselling author who loves coffee, thinks green Skittles are the best, and prefers to stay in every weekend. Brighton is multi-published with Berkley, St. Martin's Press, and Carina Press. She hates coffee, thinks green Skittles are the work of the devil, and has never heard of a party she didn't want to attend. Don't ask how they became such good friends or work so well together—they still haven't figured it out themselves.

www.londonhale.com